THE
DIAMOND
Thief

by SHARON GOSLING

SWITCH
PRESS

THE DIAMOND THIEF IS PUBLISHED IN 2015 BY SWITCH PRESS,
A CAPSTONE IMPRINT
1710 ROE CREST DRIVE
NORTH MANKATO, MINNESOTA 56003
WWW.SWITCHPRESS.COM

FIRST PUBLISHED IN 2013 BY CURIOUS FOX,
AN IMPRINT OF CAPSTONE GLOBAL LIBRARY LIMITED,
7 PILGRIM STREET, LONDON, EC4V 6LB
REGISTERED COMPANY NUMBER 6695582
WWW.CURIOUS-FOX.COM

TEXT © 2015 SHARON GOSLING

LIBRARY OF CONGRESS CATALOGING-IN-PUBLICATION DATA IS AVAILABLE
ON THE LIBRARY OF CONGRESS WEBSITE.
ISBN: 978-1-63079-002-8 (HARDCOVER)

SUMMARY:
NO ONE PERFORMS ON THE CIRCUS TRAPEZE LIKE 16-YEAR-OLD RÉMY BRUNEL.
BUT RÉMY ALSO LEADS ANOTHER LIFE, PROWLING THROUGH THE BACKSTREETS
OF VICTORIAN LONDON AS A JEWEL THIEF. WHEN SHE IS FORCED TO STEAL
ONE OF THE WORLD'S MOST VALUABLE DIAMONDS, SHE UNCOVERS A WORLD OF
TREACHERY AND FIENDISH PLOTS.

DESIGNER:
KAY FRASER

COVER ILLUSTRATION:
LIAM PETERS

IMAGE CREDIT:
SHUTTERSTOCK © LYNEA

PRINTED IN CHINA
052014   008082RRDF14

For Fiona, Emma, Jenni, Amanda,
Adam, Richard, Laura, and the other loyal early
readers who helped to shape Rémy's adventure.

Chapter 1

LE CIRQUE
DE LA LUNE

*R*émy took a deep breath as she stood on the edge of the narrow plunge board. Above her, the old material of the big top's roof was close enough to touch. Below her was nothing at all but air dirtied by dust and tobacco smoke, and then, sixty feet below, arranged around the sawdust of the circus ring, there was the crowd. She could almost hear their silence, the collected indrawn breath of five hundred people. They were all waiting to see what she could do. They wanted to see her tumble through the air above them, to dive and swoop, hanging from a thin metal bar suspended only by two old ropes. And perhaps . . . just perhaps, this time, she would fall.

Beside her, Larotti balanced precariously, holding her trapeze still. Rémy dipped her hands in the chalk bowl, clapping them together to send a shower of white dust raining through the flickering gaslight. Then she nodded once, chin held high. The little Italian let go as the strains of Saint-Saëns's "Danse Macabre" began to rise from the ragged little orchestra below. Rémy counted two beats as the trapeze dropped away.

Then she leapt into thin air.

For a second, there was nothing to keep her from falling to a horrible death. The crowd gasped, and then, as Rémy's fingers caught the fleeing trapeze, they sighed in relief. The sound rippled around the huge tent like a breeze, shivering its faded red and yellow stripes.

Rémy twisted lightly, graceful as a bird. She was wearing her favorite costume — it was cerise pink, edged in black, and, even though it was old and had been repaired more times than she could remember, it still stood out perfectly against her pale skin and unruly black hair. Rémy wore it with long fishnet stockings and greasepaint around her eyes, which made her look like a harlequin. Claudette had fashioned a flower from a scrap of almost-matching satin for her hair, along with two long, thin feathers dyed pitch black. From a distance, people said Rémy looked like a bird of paradise, flying on invisible wings.

She flipped herself backward, letting go of the bar with her hands and catching the trapeze with her feet instead, arms stretching down toward the sawdust. Rémy flicked her hips to the right, sending the trapeze into a fast spin as she let one foot come loose and held it straight out, so the audience could see that now, it was only by one ankle that she had any hold at all.

Slowing the spin, Rémy righted herself again, dancing up to stand on her hands on the bar before somersaulting backward as the trapeze swung in a graceful arc above the crowd.

Far below her, Rémy heard Claudette's sharp whistle echo in the distance. Glancing down, she saw Dominique canter into the sawdust circle. The little palomino wore an old tan saddle and a feather headdress to match Rémy's own, and on her back was Nicodemus. The pony circled, her pace steady as the wizened little capuchin monkey began to somersault too, over and over, copying Rémy's movements on Dominique's back. The crowd roared with laughter, pointing and clapping and slapping their thighs in delight.

Rémy swung the trapeze twice more, gathering

speed as the music built and built. She somersaulted again and again, faster and faster. Below, Nicodemus kept perfect time with her all the way.

And then, as the music reached its crescendo, she somersaulted again, twisting backward, reaching for the bar . . .

She missed. Her fingers brushed the metal of the trapeze, but they did not grip it.

Rémy fell like a stone.

Screams erupted around the big tent. People stood, shouting and pointing. Men waved their tattered hats in the air, women pulled their patched shawls up around their faces or used them to shield their children's eyes, as Rémy plunged head-first toward the compacted earth of the sawdust ring. She managed to twist in mid-air, a mighty turnabout that tipped her upright.

There was a flurry of movement in the corner of her eye. Someone from the audience had lunged over the barrier. It was a young man in a long brown coat and top hat — he was rushing toward her, arms outstretched, as if to break her fall.

Rémy's would-be rescuer was so focused on catching her that he almost stepped straight into the path of her horse. Thankfully, Dominique had seen

Rémy falling and knew what she had to do. The pony butted the man out of the way, hard enough to send him sprawling, but at least out of harm's way. Then she slowed until she was in exactly the right spot. Nicodemus jumped from her back and ran to the upturned bucket in the middle of the ring.

Rémy landed squarely, with both feet, on the pony's saddle, immediately lifting one leg to stand in ballet pose, her free foot pointing elegantly outwards. Dominique continued to canter in a circle as Rémy rode her one-footed. Still standing on the upturned bucket, Nicodemus saluted them both.

There was a second of silence as the crowd realized what had happened. And then the sound of cheering and clapping swept over Rémy like a tide, louder than for any other act that night. But then, it always was.

She dropped until she was seated on the pony's back, patting Dominique with one hand as she waved to the audience with the other. She'd usually do a couple of victory circuits of the ring to soak up the applause, but tonight Rémy's gaze searched for the man who had tried to save her. He was still picking himself up, forlornly brushing sawdust from his coat.

"Sorry," she called over the thunderous sound of the audience as she pulled Dominique to a halt beside him. "She is trained not to let anything get in her way when we do my act. If she had stopped, I would have died. And you too, probably. I would have crushed you!"

The young man looked up at her. To her surprise, she saw he couldn't be that much older than she was. It was his eyes that really startled her, though. They were two different colors — one as blue as the sky over Paris on a bright day in May, one as deep brown as good chocolate. And they twinkled.

He bent down to retrieve his hat and pushed it on over his mussed hair before replying.

"Well," he said with a slight smile. "That'll teach me to be a good Samaritan, won't it? People do keep telling me I shouldn't bother. Good day, miss."

He tipped his hat briefly and then turned away. A second later, he was lost in the crowd. Rémy's gaze tried to follow him, but it was no good. He was gone.

She and Dominique did one more circuit of the ring and then left the big top, Nicodemus skittering along in their wake.

Claudette was waiting for her at the players' entrance. The little monkey rushed off into the thick night, through London's chill drizzle and back to the animal enclosure. Claudette tutted as she saw Rémy adjust her opal necklace, pulling it down from where it had flown up around her ears as she'd fallen.

"You know you should not wear that on the wire, *ma chérie*," Claudette chided in her gentle, sing-song voice, as Rémy slid gracefully from Dominique's back. "One of these days, you will strangle yourself. And it will be a night like tonight, when someone stupid tries to save the girl who does not need to be saved."

Rémy grinned as she took the threadbare black robe Claudette held out and slipped it on over her shoulders. She kicked off the silver slippers she always wore on the trapeze and struggled into her boots instead. They were leather, black and worn like everything else she possessed, and the only pair she had owned since she was ten — six whole years. "Never, Claudette. You know me. I live a charmed life. Probably because I never take my opal off."

Claudette shook her head with long-suffering patience, her thick chestnut hair hanging loose around her shoulders. At twenty-four, she was eight years older than Rémy, and along with her little daughter, Amélie, was the closest thing Rémy had to family.

"Well, I hope your charm is at full power tonight," Claudette told her. "Gustave wants to see you."

Rémy made a face and sighed. "Ach. It must be time."

Claudette raised an eyebrow. Her eyes seemed even darker than usual, and they bore a trace of worry. "Take care, *chérie*. This one will be difficult, I think. We are not in France now, you know. This is the great city of London, not a little town in Provence."

Rémy straightened up and wiped rain from her eyes as she regarded her friend. Claudette was a fortune-teller and talented pickpocket. She could take a wallet from its owner and they would swear blind she'd never even been close enough to touch them. They were all vagabonds and thieves at Le Cirque de la Lune — and Rémy . . . well, Rémy was queen of them all. She'd been stealing since she was old enough to walk, and a jewel thief since she'd learned how to work the wire at age eight. Now, she was the best gem snatcher in Europe, probably in the whole of the world. Rémy had never been caught. *And*, she thought, *I never will be. Never.*

"You worry too much," she said. "Why should this be different to any other? They'll never catch me, Claudette. That is what makes me so valuable to Gustave, yes?"

Claudette sighed. "You should not take these things

too lightly, Rémy," she warned. "One day your luck will run out. And in any case, this life . . . it is not good enough for you. You should run, while you still can. Gustave could not —"

Rémy shook her head. "When I can take you and Amélie with me, then we will all go," she said. "But not before. We need money! And now is not the time for this old argument of ours, *ma belle amie*. I must go before the old goat gets too impatient. Kiss Amélie good night for me. Tell her she must sleep well because Dominique will be waiting to give her another lesson in the morning."

Claudette smiled, taking Dominique's reigns and digging a sugar lump from her pocket as she led her away. "Then you had better make sure you come back, hadn't you, Little Bird?"

Rémy watched Claudette disappear into the thick black shadows of the circus tents. Behind her, the last of the audience was leaving, laughing and chattering. She smiled. She had been good tonight — really good, even despite the almost-disaster caused by the boy with the mismatched eyes. Rémy was always good, she knew that, but some nights it felt as if she could walk on air, and those were always her best performances. Not that Gustave ever paid her extra, or praised her work. He was more interested in her other, illegal, skills.

Rémy looked toward his caravan. It stood apart from the rest, at the back of the field he had rented for them. Well, Gustave called it a field, but it was really just a barren patch of land behind the Spitalfields market, turned to mud by the never-ending rain. Rémy glanced up, blinking into the night gloom at the sooty gray clouds that seemed permanently gathered overhead. Out beyond the market square, the buildings of London slouched toward each other as if sheltering together from the miserable weather. Lights flickered and guttered in windows caked with grime and soot. The silhouettes of the taller townhouses of the East End loomed darkly over the cobbled streets. It was the first time Rémy had left France, and she'd expected a better, brighter place. But there was as much dirt and poverty here as at home, and the bread was bad, too. She dreamed of a life somewhere else, somewhere sunny, where she did not have to steal. One day . . .

Rémy pulled her hands into her sleeves and scuffed the toe of her boot into the mud. "One day" was not tonight, she reminded herself. Tonight, she had to steal the second biggest diamond in the world.

Squaring her shoulders, she headed for Gustave's

haunt. She could hear music from inside the caravan, and knew it was Dorffman, the German, playing his violin. He was supposed to be the circus's chief carpenter, but ever since Gustave had uncovered Dorffman's musical skills, he'd made him play every night as the circus owner ate. Rémy wondered what crime the man had committed to end up in this place. She liked him and he seemed nice, but it could be anything. Murder, maybe, although it was more likely to be theft . . . but everyone at Le Cirque de la Lune had their own story. One day she would ask, she decided, as she mounted the rickety, painted steps to her master's door.

"Come!" came the yell of his voice as she knocked.

Inside, Gustave was at his dinner, tearing a whole roast chicken apart with his fat fingers. The sight of the grease trickling down over his knuckles turned Rémy's stomach and made her forget that she hadn't eaten since lunch, and then only a round of gritty, gray bread and dripping.

The circus owner glanced up at her. "The cloud is thick tonight. It is Friday, the police are tired after their long week," he grunted. "But still, now is not the time."

She blinked, surprised. "No?"

"No," Gustave rumbled around a mouthful of food.

"You see, this is important. More important than any other job you've ever done. And so I want you to do a . . . reconnoiter. Find the best way in, determine where the guards are stationed and, more importantly, establish your escape route. Make the plan infallible, yes? You must not fail me, Rémy."

For a moment, Rémy was speechless. He'd never asked her to do reconnaissance before. And she had never, ever failed him. She had never even come close to failing.

Seeing her indignation, Gustave sighed and put down his chicken. "You know where this jewel is being kept?"

"In the Tower of London, master."

"Yes," he said, his voice dry. "The Tower of London. Make no mistake, my little thieving genius. However good you are, this is going to be the hardest thing you have ever tried. So, reconnaissance. There is to be a reception for the great and the good at the Tower tomorrow night. It is the perfect opportunity for you to learn everything you need to know about where the jewel is held. Now, tell me what you are looking for."

"The Darya-ye Noor," Rémy huffed.

"And what are you not looking for?"

"The Koh-i Noor. I know."

He snorted, sending flecks of grease and chicken flesh to pepper the table. "You think you know everything, do you not, little Rémy? Can you tell me the difference between the two?"

Rémy sighed. Gustave had been lecturing her on this for weeks. As if she couldn't tell one diamond from another. As if she hadn't been born able to know the worth of a gem just by looking at it. Rémy remembered every precious stone she'd ever seen in her life, and she could feel all of them now as if she held them still. In her hands jewels were living things, and they seemed to like her. They fell toward her fingers gratefully. She knew them. The thief toyed with the opal around her neck absently, and recited Gustave's lessons.

"The Koh-i Noor — the Mountain of Light — and the Darya-ye Noor — the Ocean of Light — are sister-stones. They were both mined from Golconda in India more than a century ago. Now Queen Victoria owns the Mountain of Light, and the Shah of Persia owns the Ocean of Light. And for the first time since they were both mined, the stones are back together. In the Tower of London. So that is why we are here."

"And what do we want?"

"The ocean, not the mountain," Rémy repeated, dutifully.

Gustave's pudgy, pasty face creased into a frown. "Remember that, Little Bird. The Ocean is smaller than the Mountain, but prettier. And it belongs to the Shah, not the Queen, so the good policemen of London will not care so much about it. Get in, take it, get out. That's what you need to do when the time is right. Do not get distracted by the larger stone. Do you understand me?"

"Yes, master."

He nodded slowly, and then held up the remains of his dinner's carcass. "Do that, and there will be one of these for you. You can share it with that light-fingered friend of yours. And her strange little whelp, if you really do insist on feeding it."

Rémy held herself still, but she wanted to hit him. How dare he talk about Amélie like that? Just because she was different, just because she didn't speak. How dare he —

"Well?" Gustave bellowed. "What are you waiting for? Go! Prepare!"

Rémy gritted her teeth and left, slamming the door as she ran down the steps. The sound was masked by Dorffman and his mournful violin, the ripple of sad strings rising into the dead, wet night.

* * *

Thaddeus reached his front door as the rain began to fall in earnest. He stuck his hand in his coat pocket, searching for his key, and then remembered that he didn't have it. It was on his desk at Scotland Yard. He'd left it there by accident earlier, when he'd been sent on yet another wild goose chase by the Chief. At the time he'd told himself he'd go back for it, but then he'd noticed that the circus had arrived in town, and . . .

With a sigh, Thaddeus looked up at the window belonging to what his landlady generously termed his "suite." It was really just one room with a water closet next to it, but it was all he could afford and at least it was close to the police station. The young policeman saw that he was out of luck — his window was shut, and most likely locked. Mrs. Carmichael was very particular about security, and very suspicious of fresh air. He looked at the door again, and the bell pull hanging beside it. It was no good — he'd have to ring it, even though getting her out of bed would probably mean a burned breakfast as punishment in the morning.

He regretted pulling the bell as soon as he heard her angry footsteps in the hallway. He should have just gone back to the station. He could have slept in his chair.

The door was wrenched open a crack. A poker, a candle, and one eye appeared around it.

"It's me, Mrs. Carmichael. I am most terribly sorry. I —"

"Mr. Rec!" The door was flung wide. His landlady crossed her arms over her nightgown and looked him up and down, eyes narrowed. "And where, might I ask, is your key?"

"On my desk," Thaddeus began again. "I'm sorry, but —"

"Your desk," repeated Mrs. Carmichael accusingly, as if he'd somehow said something disgusting. She didn't approve of his work with the police. Detecting, she had told him once, was nothing but nosing about in other people's business. It seemed that such a thing should only be done from behind one's curtains, if her habits were anything to go by. Not that he'd dared to remark as much to her.

Thaddeus stepped forward. He wanted to get out of the rain, but she didn't seem inclined to move. "May I —"

"Mr. Rec," Mrs. Carmichael said in outraged tones, as he stepped into the light. "Have you — have you been brawling?"

Thaddeus looked down at himself. He still had

sawdust clinging to his knees, his shoes were scuffed, and the sleeve of his coat arm was torn.

"Oh," he said. "No — no, of course not. I was at the circus. There was this girl, you see. She fell. Or at least, I thought she had, so I was trying to —"

Mrs. Carmichael rolled her eyes before turning away. "The circus. A girl. Of course. Heaven forbid you be anywhere reputable. Honestly, if you had a mother I would send you home for a drubbing. That'd sort you out, and no mistake. Come along, if you please, Mr. Rec. I don't want to catch a chill in that nasty night air. And besides — some of us have real work to do in the morning."

She disappeared down the hallway, taking the light of the candle with her. Thaddeus shut the door behind him and sighed as he drew the bolt before trudging up the stairs to the second floor. What an evening. He'd only gone to the circus for work. Well, for potential work, anyway. He had noticed — Thaddeus had a knack for noticing things — that the number of petty crimes always went up when the circus was in town. He'd thought it would do no harm to take a look around, especially now, with the Shah's visit. So he'd done a bit of a patrol, just to see if he could get a whiff of any shenanigans before they happened.

None of the other detectives had been willing to join him. They all thought he was too young to be part of their team anyway and mocked his ideas at every opportunity. Besides, it was time for their dinners, and it was a miserable night to be out and about. Thaddeus had gone anyway, alone. He'd been standing outside the big top making notes when he'd heard a whisper that the final act was the most amazing anyone had ever seen. *Astounding*, the whisper had said. *Not to be missed. He'd stuck his head inside, just out of curiosity.*

And there she was. A girl who seemed to fly without wings, as perfectly as a bird. He'd been instantly fascinated and couldn't help pushing his way to a seat in the front row, just to watch her. And when she'd fallen —

Even the thought of it made his heart freeze in his chest. The memory of her plummeting to the ground was horrifying. Before he'd known what he was doing, he'd been over the barrier and running, desperate to catch her . . . to save her.

The door to his room clicked shut behind him and Thaddeus leaned against it, raising his eyes to the ceiling. Of course it was a trick. They were circus folk — their whole lives were about tricks. He should have known better. She probably had a wire attached so she couldn't reach the ground anyway, for goodness sake. What a fool! She was probably laughing at him right now, standing around the campfire with the rest of them. Still, he wondered who she was and where she had come from. He thought her accent had been French, but he couldn't be sure over the noise of the crowd. And she spoke such good English. Where had she learned that? He'd looked for the posters outside, but on the line for her act all it said was "Little Bird."

Shaking himself, Thaddeus pushed away from the door and glanced at his clock, ticking away quietly on the mantel. It was almost one in the morning, but he knew he wouldn't sleep.

Thaddeus glanced at his workbench. On it were the night glasses he'd been working on with the Professor — their latest joint invention. Thaddeus was convinced that a modern police force needed modern machines, and his friend the Professor agreed with him. He wasn't really a professor — that had just been his nickname ever since Thaddeus had known him. In fact, Thaddeus wasn't even sure what the man's real name was, as for some reason, the Professor preferred people not to know. He was a mechanical genius and ever since they'd met, he and Thaddeus had shared their ideas for weird and wonderful gadgets.

The night glasses, though — they were another level of brilliance altogether. If they managed to perfect their invention, Thaddeus and the Professor believed that they could make it possible to see in the dark, just as if it were day, even if a person was in a pitch-black room. If they got it right, the darkest corners of London's dingiest streets and dens would be visible to the police. It would be a revolution.

The glasses weren't perfect yet, but they would be soon. In fact, Thaddeus had been hoping they'd be ready for the Shah's arrival. The other coppers kept insisting that the Koh-i Noor and the Darya-ye Noor were "as safe as houses" inside the Tower, but Thaddeus wasn't so sure. The gems weren't being kept in the Jewel House, which was specially reinforced. Queen Victoria wanted to make a proper occasion out of the visit, and had decreed that both stones be put on display in the Long Hall. It made Thaddeus very nervous indeed, especially since Her Majesty had also decided to throw a week of receptions for the richest and most important people in the land to show off the jewels.

None of the other men in the city's detective division were concerned — they just laughed when he brought up the idea that someone would try to steal one or both of the jewels. No one believed that anyone could break into the great Tower of London, and even if they did, the place was crawling with police and Tower guards, watching the gems every moment of every day.

But Thaddeus just had a feeling. A hunch, you could call it. It had been keeping him awake for weeks, through all the preparations for the Shah's visit. And now that the gems were here, in London . . .

He shrugged off his damp coat. Sitting down at his workbench, he lit the Bunsen burner. It wasn't really that late, after all. He could do a little more work on the glasses. Maybe he could get them working properly in time for the first reception tomorrow.

As he worked, the night ticked onwards into day.

Chapter 2

IN PLAIN SIGHT

"*I* am not wearing that!"

Claudette, kneeling on the floor of her caravan, looked up at Rémy with raised eyebrows. Morning sunlight from the open windows dappled her face. "And why not? What is wrong with it?"

"It is . . . it is . . ." Rémy threw her hands into the air. "A dress! A long one!"

Her friend sighed and pushed another pin into place on the hem of the old gown before standing up to admire her handiwork. "Well done. I was not at all sure you knew what such a thing was."

Rémy crossed her arms. "It's horrible . . . and uncomfortable. I won't wear it."

"So what? You are going to walk into this reception — a reception that the Queen of England
herself may be at — looking like the ragamuffin
orphan that you are?" Claudette pointed to Rémy's
current outfit — a pair of tattered trousers that
were too short, coupled with a rough blouse and
belt. "This is not how young women usually dress,
Rémy."

"It's stupid," Rémy said, sulkily, "all of it. Why does
he want to make me do this, anyway? As if I do not
know what I'm doing."

"Well, I for one am glad, *ma chérie*. I think once you
go there, you will realize that what Gustave asks is the
right thing. For once. Now, try it on. I need to see if I
have fitted it correctly."

"No."

Claudette tutted. "You are forgetting the good side
of having so many skirts, Little Bird."

Rémy frowned. As far as she could see, the only
thing that skirts did was stop you from running away
properly. "What do you mean?"

Claudette lifted the wine-colored material to show
one of the petticoats underneath. She had stitched
several pockets into it, and pointed to each one. "Lock-
picks. Rope. Penknife. Scarf . . ."

Rémy stared and then began to laugh. "Very well," she said. "I will try it your way. Just this once."

Claudette smiled, satisfied. "And what will you say? Once you get to the door? How will you make them let you in?"

Rémy shrugged. "I have not quite worked that out yet. But I'm sure I'll think of something."

★ ★ ★

Later, Rémy stood in the Long Hall, slightly stunned by the rich swirl of music and the beauty of the noblemen and noblewomen that filled the room. She looked down at herself and was suddenly relieved that Claudette's nimble fingers were as quick and sure with a needle as they were with a stranger's wallet. She felt out of place, but at least she didn't look it.

Rémy looked down at the old man whose hand was still tucked into the crook of her elbow. He had been her ticket into the Tower. She had arrived at the gate imagining that entry would be, if not easy, then at least not impossible. If she couldn't get through the gate, Rémy thought, she could find a wall low enough to scale even in the long skirts that swamped her agile legs. She'd simply join the reception inside by a more circuitous route. But the imposing sight of the Tower had stopped her dead. The thick walls seemed to be layered, each against the other, higher and higher, and each more impervious than the one before. The stones were rough, yes, but there was no hope of climbing them. Vast pools of flickering light from the huge, burning torches pinned to the walls created some shadows, but not nearly enough.

She'd been contemplating her options when a carriage had driven up, the footman jumping down to help an old man onto the uneven roadway leading to the gate. He was dressed in a fine suit and shook off the attentions of his servant, despite his obvious need of help. And so Rémy, in a flash of inspiration, had offered her arm. She had learned early that old men will take help from young women far more easily than from other men. She walked with him to the gate, heart beating a fearful pattern despite her outward smiles. The old man chattered away in his ancient voice — he enjoyed her accent, he told her; it added an extra air of refinement to a young lady of good breeding, such as herself. Still, the guard who stopped them at the gate obviously hadn't been as sure of her "breeding."

"Tickets, please," he'd said suspiciously.

She'd pretended to search her pockets. "I . . . I must have left mine inside," she stuttered with feigned confusion. "I came out, you see — for some fresh air. If you just let me in, I will find my father . . ."

The guard shook his head. "No entry without tickets. Sir?"

The old man had presented his own invitation and was glowering at the guard.

"My Lord," the guard corrected immediately, as he looked at the name on the ticket. "My apologies, Lord Abernathy, I did not realize . . ."

"This young lady is with me," her companion had said firmly. "Honestly man, don't you know who this is?" Lord Abernathy had turned to her, a slight twinkle in his eye, and just for a moment Rémy wondered whether, somehow, he knew what she was really up to. "Tell him, my dear," he'd urged. "He will soon regret his rudeness."

"I . . . I am Rémy Brunel," she said, raising her chin as if she were on the wire. "Of Cordes-sur-Ciel. I am here with my father, and . . ."

"That is enough, my dear." Lord Abernathy had raised an eyebrow at the guard. "Well, my lad?"

The guard looked her up and down again, but obviously wasn't keen to raise the wrath of a lord.

"Very well. Welcome to the Tower of London, Lord Abernathy, my lady . . . Brunel. Enjoy your evening."

And so it was that Rémy, for the first — and probably the last time in her life — had entered a room on the arm of a lord.

"Can I get something for you, my Lord?" she asked now. "A glass of wine? Water? A chair?"

He smiled again, rheumy eyes still blue enough to twinkle, and shook his head. "My dear," he said, "I am sure you have other places you would prefer to be. Thank you for your kind assistance, but I do not expect your company to persist for the entire evening. Go now. Enjoy yourself. Perhaps I will see you later. And give my regards to your father."

Rémy curtsied. "I will be sure to. Good evening, my Lord."

When she straightened, Lord Abernathy was already making his way, feebly, through the throng of people. Rémy turned away, surveying the crowded room. In fact, the Long Hall was not just one room but two, connected by a wide corridor that had been added in the past century. The alteration had created a large, long gallery of whitewashed walls and polished wooden floors, with the two rooms at either end providing larger spaces for guests to mill about in. It was in each of these rooms that the famed diamonds had been exhibited, facing each other at either end. Rémy wanted to look at both stones, but knew she had to concentrate on the Darya-ye Noor. She approached the small crowd gathered around it, patiently waiting her turn until she had made her way to the front.

It was worth the wait. The Shah of Persia's Ocean of Light stole Rémy's breath with her first glimpse. It was large — the largest Rémy had ever seen — and cut into a pillow shape. It was the Ocean's color, though, that really took Rémy by surprise. She had been expecting it to be clear, translucent, or perhaps the pale yellow of champagne that some good diamonds were. But the Darya-ye Noor instead shone a delicate and beautiful rose pink, enhanced by the black velvet pillow on which it lay. Rémy was hypnotized by the diamond's shine, by the way it reflected every flicker of light that came its way in a halo of miniature rainbows.

The jostling around her snapped Rémy out of her daydream. She was here to work and could not afford to delay. Gustave was still expecting her back for the finale performance tonight. He knew that the crowd was mostly there to see her act, and besides, her nightly turn on the high wire was good cover for her other activities. How could she be a thief if she was performing every night in front of hundreds?

Rémy quickly ran her eyes over the stone's surroundings. It was enclosed by a glass case on a black marble plinth. The stone and its pillow stood on a small mechanical pillar that had been built to rotate. Its cogs and gears were clearly visible beneath the velvet, working to constantly turn the stone to the light. Rémy leaned closer, wondering if the clockwork mechanism hid some kind of alarm bell that would sound when the stone was removed, but she could see nothing of the kind.

An elbow dug into her ribs — the hopeful admirers behind her were becoming impatient. Rémy turned and made her way out of the scrum. She'd seen what she needed to of the stone's housing. Now she had to work out how to penetrate the Tower itself.

It wouldn't be easy, that was for sure. Even once she was inside the outer wall — and at the moment Rémy had no idea how she would achieve that feat — she'd have to find a way into the Long Hall. She looked up. The two rooms that housed the exhibits had flat ceilings interrupted only by ornate carvings. But the corridor that connected them was partly gabled with a flat center. Looking up, Rémy could see skylights in the highest part of the roof, large enough that the smoky clouds of London were visible above the glass.

One of them was open, letting fresh air into the stuffy reception. Rémy wove through the knots of guests toward Queen Victoria's diamond, looking up at those distant windows. They'd be too high for most people to consider, but for her . . .

By the time she had reached the other end of the corridor, she had decided. That was her way into the stone room. Now all she had to do was see what was up there on the roof and work out how to get into the tower itself.

Rémy had been so absorbed in her contemplation of the skylights that at first she didn't notice the change in guests as she approached the Koh-i Noor. But, suddenly, Rémy became aware of cautious eyes scanning the crowd. She retired to the edge of the room, deftly collecting a glass of champagne from one of the silver trays being offered by the Tower's liveried butlers. As she sipped, she watched. Yes — in this part of the hall she could count at least twenty police officers, trying their best to blend in as they surreptitiously watched the guests. She'd seen none surrounding the Shah of Persia's diamond. Gustave had been right again. It was the Mountain they were protecting, not the Ocean.

Rémy looked up at the skylights again, wondering

how sturdy the roof was. She needed to find out, since it seemed to her that it would be the only way in.

Slipping out of the Long Hall, Rémy moved quickly. She had to find the servants' passageways — there must be an exit to the roof somewhere, but it would be for the staff only. Someone must have opened that window, after all — it would be impossible to do from the inside, even with a very long pole. She entered a quiet corridor. About halfway along, she found a door, its plain wooden surface disturbed only by a keyhole. Rémy stood still for a moment, listening to the low burble of chatter from the Long Hall, but all seemed silent beyond the door.

Quickly, she hitched up the outer layer of her dress, and pulled her lock-picks from the pocket Claudette had added to her petticoat. Gustave had taught her how to pick a lock when she was six years old, and Rémy still had the pick set he'd given her then. It was old and worn, but it still worked. She crouched down, peering at the lock. The trick when lock-picking, Gustave had told her, was not in the pushing of the pins, but the amount of pressure you applied to the plug. Too much, and the plates inside wouldn't align, even if you managed to push all the pins up. But just enough, and . . .

Rémy felt the plug turn, a suddenly smooth motion of polished metal against polished metal. The plates aligned with a tiny *click*, and the door swung open, revealing darkness beyond.

There was a sudden burst of laughter from further down the corridor, and the sound of loud voices and louder footsteps. Someone was coming! Rémy scrambled to her feet, the heels of her boots snagging on the skirts of her dress. She wrenched the picks from the lock and slipped through the door, pushing it shut behind her and standing as still as she could, holding her breath. The voices passed, their owners too intent on their merry conversation to notice anything amiss.

Sighing in relief, Rémy turned. She was in a dull, narrow passageway, one that no noble man or woman would ever see — it was built only for the servants. And there, around another corner, was a flight of steps leading up.

Rémy emerged onto the Tower's roof and into heavy darkness. She made her way toward the faint glow of the skylights, picking up her skirts to move more easily.

From above, the distance to the floor of the hall looked further, although it couldn't have been more than thirty feet — less than she flew every night on the trapeze. Leaning over the skylight, Rémy examined its locks. They were firm but did not close with a key, which wasn't surprising. Who would try to break in from up here? Who would even get this far? Rémy looked around. If she were going to do this — and it would be the only way — she'd need to be able get out again. She'd have to secure a rope . . .

The sound of metal clanging against metal startled her into fear. Voices broke into the cold night air and Rémy spun in the direction of her escape route — someone had followed her up the stairs!

Rémy ducked into the shadows, her heart pounding. At least she had the night on her side. Up here, the only light came from the weak moon and the meager shine rising through the glass of the skylights. She held her breath, hoping that whoever it was had just needed a breath of fresh air and would soon go away.

"What a worrier," grunted a man's gruff voice. "I'm telling you, there's no one up here."

"I saw a shadow," said another, firmly. Rémy recognized this voice somehow, though she wasn't sure where from. "I'm sure I saw someone peering through the open skylight."

"You're losing it, Rec," said the other man. There

came the sound of someone rubbing their hands together. "It's freezing up here!"

"Would you rather the diamonds were stolen on our watch?" asked the familiar voice.

There was an impatient sigh. "No one's going to steal anything from here, boy. This place is a fortress. Come on then, Thaddeus," the voice added. "You've been going on about these glasses of yours for weeks, so you might as well get 'em out. What's they all about, anyway?"

Rémy strained to see out of her hiding place. The two men were slowly moving closer, but it was too dark for them to be clear.

"You'll see," came the soft voice again. "This is going to revolutionize detective work, Collins. These will let me see in the dark, just as if it were day."

Detective work? They were policemen!

There was a pause. Despite her fear, Rémy craned her neck, trying to see what was happening. There was a sudden guffaw of laughter.

"Well," chortled Collins. "It'll give us a laugh, at any rate. You'll look like a clown if you put those on, Rec. You should go and join that circus of yours. They'd have you like a shot!"

The circus? Rémy thought, startled. *Why would they*

mention the circus? Then the moon cleared a patch of cloud and the two men passed into light, just for a moment. She clamped a hand over her mouth to cut off a gasp as she recognized one of them.

It was the man from last night! The one who had tried to save her!

"You can laugh," she heard him say, "but just you wait. You'll see. There was someone up here, I swear. And with these, I'll be able to see them, even in the dark. The shadow passed right overhead — over there, by that skylight."

The footsteps became louder, nearer. Rémy peered from her hiding place, and her heart stopped altogether. The boy with the mismatched eyes had put on the strangest pair of glasses she had ever seen.

And he was looking straight at her.

{*Chapter 3*}

SLEIGHT OF HAND

$\mathcal{T}$he moon passed once more into shadow, casting the corner where Rémy crouched into an even deeper darkness. She dared not move. Had he seen her? The boy with the odd eyes — Thaddeus, his companion had called him, Thaddeus Rec — had seemed to be staring right at her. But how could he have seen anything in this gloom?

Seconds seemed to stretch into hours. Rémy thought the two policemen were about to move toward her. But then, suddenly, the silence of the night was split by a loud crash, followed by the piercing sound of an alarm bell. It came from below, exploding through the open skylight from the Long Hall.

"What the bleedin' 'eck is that?" shouted Collins over the noise.

"It's the alarm on the jewel case," Rémy heard Thaddeus reply. He sounded panicked. "Quick — let's get back down there!"

Rémy peered after them as they rushed back to the steps, her heart pounding. Surely someone hadn't beaten her to it and stolen one of the diamonds already? The moment she heard the door leading inside clang shut, she scrambled out of her hiding place and ran to the skylight, taking care not to lean far enough over to be seen from below.

The alarm fell abruptly silent, but below she could see a scene of total chaos. The plinth bearing the Darya-ye Noor had been knocked over and lay in pieces on the floor, the glass case housing the diamond smashed to smithereens. Guests were gathered around it in a wide circle, pushing forward and chattering loudly as guards and policemen in plain clothes tried to hold them back. In the middle, spread out on the floor, his head touching the fallen plinth as if he had collided with it, lay the old man who had unwittingly helped Rémy get into the Tower — Lord Abernathy. Of the Ocean of Light, though, there was no sign.

"Let me help him!" shouted a voice from the crowd.

"He's an old man, and he's clearly ill. I'm a doctor, let me through!"

"Let him through, you brutes!" called a lady dressed in a beautiful, rich-looking dress. "The old man needs help, can't you see?" A murmur of angry agreement passed through the crowd, and the doctor was duly let through. He knelt beside Abernathy, holding two fingers to his pulse and nodding to himself.

Rémy watched as Thaddeus and Collins entered the fray, pushing through the crowd until they reached one of the other policemen — a large, portly man in a tailcoat, who seemed to be in charge and who was standing directly below Rémy.

"Ah, Rec, there you are," Rémy heard him say, over the noise of the crowd. "It's all right, nothing to panic about. It's not a burglary, just an accident. Lord Abernathy has been taken ill. He fell against the exhibit, breaking the glass."

"And the Shah of Persia's diamond, Chief Inspector?" Thaddeus asked urgently. "Is it safe?"

"Quite safe," the other man answered. He stepped closer to Thaddeus, leaning in as he muttered something in the younger policeman's ear. There was a flurry of activity between them as the Chief Inspector quickly pushed something into Thaddeus's hand. It would have been hidden from sight to anyone closer, but from her vantage point directly above, Rémy caught sight of a sliver of gleaming jewel through the policeman's fingers. The diamond! Rémy watched as Rec slid it into the inside pocket of his coat, glancing around to make sure no one had seen. He nodded briefly at the Chief Inspector, who stepped back and turned to the crowd. "Now, now, ladies and gentlemen, please let Lord Abernathy have some air."

Rémy sat back on her heels, relieved. The diamond was safe — she would have another chance to steal it. There was no point staying in the Tower now, though. Better to slip out while the chaos was still at its height — no one would take any notice of one person leaving. They were all too busy tending to Lord Abernathy, or chattering about his fall and the fright it had given them.

Unseen, Rémy slipped back down the servants' stairs and out into the corridor. Everyone was still inside the Long Hall, their excited babble echoing eerily through the stone passageways of the great Tower.

She was heading for the steps that led to the exit when a voice rose above the confusion in the exhibition room.

"Rémy," it called. "Rémy Brunel?"

Rémy stopped, her heart somersaulting in her chest. She paused, wondering what to do. Her instinct told her to run, but Gustave's lessons held her still. *Running makes you look guilty*, he used to say. *Walk, don't run. No one looks twice at someone walking.*

She forced herself to stay calm and move on at a steady pace, despite the fear that prickled along her spine.

"Rémy Brunel?" the voice called again. "Is there one called Rémy Brunel among us? Lord Abernathy asks for you."

Rémy stopped again, cursing under her breath. The old man! She should have known. But . . . if she didn't come to his aid when called, wouldn't they start looking for her, wondering where she was and why she hadn't stepped forward to help?

Taking a deep breath, Rémy turned back toward the Long Hall. Part of her wanted to help the old man, anyway. He'd been kind to her earlier, and he was alone. She could at least help him to his carriage — and on his arm, no one would think to question her as she left.

Squaring her shoulders, Rémy raised her chin. She headed into the crowded gallery and began to make her way through the throng of people.

"I am Rémy Brunel," she said. "Did you ask for me?"

The crowd parted, murmuring her name as they ushered her to the front. The doctor was still kneeling beside Lord Abernathy, though Rémy could see that the old man's eyes were now open. He looked pale and ashen, his eyes watery. The doctor looked up and then motioned her forward.

"Lord Abernathy wishes for your help, miss. He says he needs no one else."

"Of course," she said. "I am happy to help. But should Lord Abernathy be moved so soon? Surely he should rest a while?"

"I'm fine," rasped the old man, struggling to sit up. "Just a little embarrassed and sore. All I need is an arm to guide me to my carriage, if you would, my dear."

Rémy nodded and knelt beside the doctor. "Can you stand, sir?" she asked.

"*Humph*. I may need a little help in that department. That's more manhandling than a young maiden like yourself should have to deal with. Doctor?"

"Of course, of course." The doctor lifted one of Lord Abernathy's arms around his shoulders.

Rémy risked a quick glance at the circle of people around them. Her eyes fell on Thaddeus Rec, standing a short distance away. He looked preoccupied. His brow was creased in a frown above his double-cultured eyes, his attention elsewhere — probably on the valuable burden within his pocket. An idea flew into Rémy's brain. Another of Gustave's interminable lessons . . .

Never waste an opportunity.

She knew where the Ocean of Light was right now. Not on an alarmed plinth, under a guarded glass shield, in an impenetrable tower. It was there, in that policeman's pocket, not six feet from where she stood.

She stood up, quick as a flash. "Sir?" she said, directing her words at Thaddeus Rec. "Would you be so kind?" She indicated the doctor, who was struggling to lift Lord Abernathy.

Rec hesitated for a split second, staring at her before his frown turned into a flush of embarrassment. "Oh, of course. Forgive me . . ." He stepped forward, brushing past Rémy as he stooped to help Lord Abernathy to his feet.

Rémy wasn't as skilled a pickpocket as Claudette, but she knew the basics. The first rule was to make sure that the target's attention was elsewhere. The second was to not hesitate. The third was to be quick as lightning.

Rémy leaned in as the policeman passed her, close enough that she could feel the warmth of his body beneath his long, heavy coat. His skin smelled of soap, the clean, sharp scent filling her lungs along with something else — something deeper, something beautiful, like the earth after rain.

Rémy's fingers slipped into Thaddeus's inner pocket, her fingers brushing against the smooth, faceted surface of the stone. A split second more and the Ocean was hers. She crouched beside Lord Abernathy's helpers, slipping the diamond beneath her ruffled skirts and into one of Claudette's handy pockets before they had even begun to lift the old man.

"Careful," she said, pretending to fuss. "Are you sure you are quite well enough, Lord Abernathy?"

"I am quite, quite well," murmured the old man, as he found himself on his feet. "Now, if you will just lend me your arm, my dear." He waved the young policeman aside, reaching a feeble hand for Rémy.

"Wait . . ."

It was Rec's voice. He was standing just behind her but Rémy pretended not to have heard.

"Don't I — don't I know you from somewhere, miss?"

It was no good. She couldn't ignore him entirely.

Rémy turned her head to see Thaddeus looking at her intently. *Those eyes*, she thought. *It's as if he can see right through me . . . As if he knows . . .*

"I am sorry — do you mean me?" she asked calmly, though her throat was dry with fear.

He looked at her a moment more and then frowned, shaking his head. "Sorry, no. I must be mistaken. Forgive me."

Rémy bowed her head, accepting his apology the way a lady would. Lord Abernathy squeezed her arm, and they left as swiftly as the old man could muster. It was nowhere near fast enough for Rémy's liking.

★ ★ ★

Thaddeus watched as Lord Abernathy and his pretty helper left the Long Hall. The girl — Rémy — he could not shake the feeling that he had seen her face before. He'd thought it was the face of the girl he had tried to save, though she had not needed saving — the devious Little Bird of Le Cirque de la Lune.

It would be hard to forget her, he had thought at the time, despite the fact that her face had been mostly hidden by elaborate greasepaint. Even so, her eyes had been so bright, like this girl's, and shone from beneath such rich black hair. But what would a circus nymph be doing here, now, on the arm of a British lord? Clearly this elegant young woman could not be part of that shabby outfit. No, he must have been mistaken — confused by their similar accents, perhaps. After all, he'd only seen the girl on the wire from a distance, and then in a flurry of embarrassment as he'd picked himself up from the floor. The idea of her was just lingering in his thoughts, that was all, though he wasn't sure why.

Even so, Thaddeus touched his hand against his outer pocket, instinctively feeling for the diamond that Chief Inspector Glove had handed him. He felt its weight there, and the knowledge of it being there pressed against his chest as heavily as the stone itself. The sooner he could pass it back to the Tower Guards and a secure resting place, the better. For the moment, though, they were all occupied with slowly ushering the guests out of the gallery. And at least no one knew where the stone had been secreted — the perfect hiding place, the Chief Inspector had said. Even the other policemen would never suspect that he would entrust the diamond to the youngest detective in the room.

Rec looked up at the skylight, where he had fancied he'd seen someone's shadow earlier. But there seemed to be no one on the roof — unless his night glasses had not been working, which was, if he were honest, a distinct possibility.

Thaddeus froze. A cold, awful wave of fear washed over him. His night glasses. He usually tucked them into his top pocket as they fitted better there, the multiple lenses didn't rattle together so much. He felt for them there now — but in his rush to get down from the roof, he must have thrust them somewhere else . . . somewhere easier to get at . . .

He patted his coat pocket again, the one he had just checked and the one he thought he had put the diamond into. With trembling fingers, Thaddeus slipped his hand inside, hoping to feel the stone's cold hardness under his fingers. But instead, his hand touched something that rattled. His glasses! There they were. The weight he had felt when he checked for the jewel wasn't the stone at all. It was his night glasses! Of course he wouldn't put such a valuable jewel in his outer pocket. He had put it in the pocket inside. His heart in his mouth, Thaddeus reached into his inner pocket.

There was nothing there.

Frantically, Thaddeus felt about, desperately hoping that the diamond was somehow hiding in a corner. He turned around on the spot, searching the floor with his eyes, as if the gem might have fallen out and was lying somewhere among the many pairs of feet now trooping homeward. But no, the Ocean of Light was nowhere to be seen — or felt.

He almost stumbled to his knees, feeling the blood rush from his face. He had lost the Shah of Persia's diamond! He had lost the Darya-ye Noor!

"Rec?" he heard a voice ask. It was Collins at his elbow, a frown on his face. "What the devil is the matter, boy? You looks as if you've seen a ghost."

Thaddeus tried to breathe. "The diamond," he managed, hoarsely. "It's gone. The diamond has gone!"

"What?" Collins frowned. "Don't be daft. It's safe, the Chief Inspector said so. You 'eard 'im yourself, Thaddeus."

Thaddeus shook his head, vigorously, his world crumbling around his ears. "He gave it to me. For safekeeping, because no one knew . . . He gave it to me, and . . ."

Her face flashed in front of his eyes, pale skin under black hair, long and elegant fingers fussing over Lord Abernathy.

"She took it!" he whispered under his breath.

"What was that?" Collins asked, eyeing Thaddeus skeptically. "What are you talking ab—"

But before he could finish, Thaddeus had begun to run toward the exit, fighting his way through the crowds and shouting, "Stop them! Stop them at once!"

Collins followed, puffing along behind him. But by the time Thaddeus made it outside, there was no sign of Lord Abernathy's carriage or of the girl called Rémy Brunel.

Chapter 4

A JADE'S TRICK

Claudette was waiting for Rémy when she got back to the circus field.

"You are very nearly late!" her friend scolded as she ran into the shadow of the big top. "I was about to send in the clowns — the crowd is becoming restless!"

As if on cue, the audience inside the tent began to stamp their feet — just a few at first, but then more and more, in unison. The woody thump echoed in the cold night air. Hauling off her gown, Rémy quickly pulled on the costume Claudette held out instead — a yellow one this time, not Rémy's favorite, but an old faithful — and slipped into her silver slippers.

"It was worth it, believe me," she said, pushing

the stolen gem into Claudette's hand. "Take that to Gustave, will you? I will go see him myself once I am off the wire."

Claudette looked down at the stone in her palm. It glittered weakly in the poor light. "What is it?"

"What do you think?"

Her friend's eyes widened. "You were not supposed to steal it tonight! You were supposed to wait!"

Rémy ignored Claudette's protests and, with a final dab of greasepaint, ran for the big top's entrance. "Tell Amélie we shall have a good dinner tonight!"

She was up on the trapeze in a trice. Rémy flew better than she had in weeks, fired up by the bravery of her theft and by the shouts of the crowd below, whose anger soon turned to delight when they saw her. She swooped and dived, spun and soared like a wonder through the smoke-fogged air. The trapeze was her freedom, and she danced with it, happily.

If she hadn't been so absorbed in her performance, she would have looked down to see two of London's policemen enter and then look up at her. She would have seen them talk, the portly one shaking his head and shrugging his shoulders as the other tried to convince him that the girl on the trapeze had been at the Tower of London moments earlier.

She would then have seen the portly one leave, stalking out of the big top muttering that the young detective was a lunatic and that his time had been wasted.

But she didn't see any of that, just as she didn't see Thaddeus Rec slip out of the tent and head for the caravans where the circus folk lived. Rémy thought only of the fact that she had done as Gustave had ordered and now they could go home to France, where at least the weather was better even if the food was still scarce. Perhaps she would have earned enough money to leave Le Cirque de la Lune behind forever.

It was these thoughts that preoccupied her as she rode her last victory lap with Dominique twenty minutes later, and exited the circus tent on a wave of thunderous applause. Claudette was waiting for her, as always — but this time her face was grave.

"Claudette?" Rémy asked. "Is something wrong? Why do you look so serious? Surely we have reason enough to celebrate tonight? Where is Amélie? She must be hungry, yes?"

Claudette shook her head. "Go see Gustave, Rémy. And I warn you — I have not seen him this angry before. Be careful, Little Bird."

"Angry?" Rémy asked, astonished. "How can he be

angry? Not with me, surely? I have done everything he asked. I have —"

"Not everything, Rémy," Claudette said softly. "Go, now, before you give him more reasons for fury."

Thinking her friend must have misunderstood their master's mood, Rémy did as she was told. Gustave's caravan was in darkness, and this time there was no sign of Dorffman or his mournful violin. She knocked on the door and then let herself in, finding the circus master sitting at his table in a gloom lessened by a single candle. The weak flame cast sharp, flickering shadows around the walls. It made the space seem smaller somehow, as if the caravan had shrunk since her last visit.

Rémy sniffed, hoping for the aroma of chicken, but there was nothing but the faint smell of damp, covered by a stronger stench of the thick red wine that Gustave liked to drink.

"Master?" she asked, puzzled by his silence. "I am just off the wire. Did Claudette bring you the stone?"

Gustave looked up at her, his dark eyes hooded. Rémy glanced at his hand and realized that he held the diamond in his palm.

"Lock the door," Gustave growled, and she obeyed,

pulling the heavy bolt across the door. "Now, is this the stone you gave to Claudette?" he asked quietly.

Rémy nodded. "Is it not magnificent?"

Gustave tossed the gem toward her, across the table. It clunked heavily as it hit the rough wooden surface, turning over once to lie, dull and still, in front of Rémy.

"It is a fake," Gustave said, his voice low and very, very dangerous.

Rémy stopped breathing. Her hearing buzzed, as if someone had slapped her hard. She was so shocked she could not move, not even to shake her head.

"No," she managed at last, the word barely heard in the thick silence gathering in the shadows around her.

"Yes," said Gustave. "You have brought me a worthless lump of glass. As worthless as you yourself are, Rémy Brunel. I trusted you. I told you what to do. And you failed me."

"No," said Rémy again, stronger this time. "No. No — it cannot be possible. It cannot!"

Gustave waved his fat finger at the stone between them. "Pick it up, oh great knower of gems. Tell me that is the world's second most valuable diamond."

Rémy reached out with trembling fingers. She held it in her palm and felt the dread grow heavy in her heart. The stone looked lifeless. There was no light in its glitter, no fire, only reflection. It was as dead as the drinking glass that held Gustave's deep red wine.

"I don't . . . I don't understand . . ." she stammered. "How can this be?"

"How?" Gustave bellowed, suddenly slamming his hand down on the table with a crack so loud that Rémy jumped. "I'll tell you how, Little Bird. You have been fooled. A jade's trick. They are not showing the real stones. The exhibition is only of fakes."

"No," Rémy said, trying desperately to understand what was happening. "That is not so. The stone I saw in the glass case — it was real. I swear it. I — I have never seen another diamond like it. It was real."

"Then explain!" Gustave roared, "Explain to me how we are sitting here now, with a fake stone!"

Rémy shook her head. "I don't know."

"What were you doing, taking it tonight, anyway?" Gustave went on, standing up and beginning to pace, his bulk filling the small caravan almost to the ceiling. "I told you to reconnoiter only. I expected you to confirm that the diamond being displayed was real, and to find a way to get in and out quietly without anyone noticing. No alarm bells, no witnesses. Do you remember my instructions?"

"Yes," said Rémy, faintly, still dazed and staring at the lacking gem, "but I saw an opportunity. The stone was out of its casing. It was . . . it was there for the taking, in his pocket . . ."

"In whose pocket?"

"In . . . in the policeman's pocket. Thaddeus Rec. He had it . . . in his pocket."

Gustave looked at Rémy as if she had gone completely mad. "You took this from a policeman's pocket?"

Rémy wasn't listening, still trying to piece together what had happened. Lord Abernathy had fallen, and the stone's case had been cracked. The Chief Inspector must have picked it up, and then she'd seen him give it to Thaddeus. It was as simple as that. The diamond had been real in the case, but not when she had taken it from his pocket. Did he have another hidden in there? Had it been a double bluff? No, surely not. Then how?

"Lord Abernathy," she whispered.

Gustave stopped pacing, his back to her. He turned, slowly. "What did you say?"

"He . . . he was taken ill," Rémy went on, hardly hearing her master. "He fell against the plinth — he set the alarm off. It was his fault that the diamond was in the policeman's pocket . . ." Rémy's thoughts ran wild. "But he was just an old man. He couldn't even walk without my help. And he was a lord! He couldn't . . . he couldn't have switched them . . ."

But could it really be true? Could Lord Abernathy have been playacting all along, fooling everyone — fooling her, the best gem thief in the world? Had he faked his illness and swapped the stone?

Gustave leaned over her, close enough that she could smell the old sweat that had dried on his flabby jowls. "Tell me," he said, softly, clearly, with enough menace to freeze the blood. "What name? Say it again."

"Lord Abernathy," Rémy repeated. "He . . . he helped me. If not for him, I wouldn't have been able to get into the Tower at all. He was an old man . . ."

Gustave made a harsh sound in his throat and straightened up. "Abernathy," he growled, rolling the name around his tongue until it sounded like a clap of thunder in his mouth. "A-ber-na-thy."

Rémy blinked. "You . . . you know of him?"

The circus master looked down at her, his dark eyes glinting angrily. "Know of him? Oh yes, I dare say. I knew an Abernathy once. But he was no lord of Great Britain. He was not an old man, either. You have been duped, my girl — twice. You fool, Rémy! And now, what do I do with you? Once Abernathy talks to the police and casts suspicion on you — telling them how he had never met you before, how you used him to access the tower — the police will hunt you down. They would never suspect him, of course! He has committed the perfect crime. And you . . . you took this from a police-man's pocket! Surrounded by prying eyes! Idiot child!"

Rémy shook her head. "Then . . . then we'll pack up. We can leave, tonight. Go back to France, before anyone can stop us."

Gustave bared his teeth. "And what," he asked softly, "of the Ocean of Light?"

She frowned. "There — there are other stones, many others, all easier to steal. I can make this up to you, Gustave. I will steal more, once we are back in France — much more, whatever you want —"

Gustave roared again, swinging his hand to slap her soundly across the cheek. The blow was so hard and so painful that Rémy was almost knocked clean out of her chair. Her eyes watered with shock and tears.

"There is no other diamond!" Gustave bellowed. "I must have that one! I must! Foolish child! I should have sent Nicodemus. Perhaps his paws would have been more reliable than your fingers!"

Gustave looked down at her, a flash of disgust in his eyes. "I should have known that you would fail, just as your parents did before you," he said.

"My . . . my parents! What do you mean? What do you know about them?" she stammered, all the while clutching nervously at the opal around her neck. "I don't understand."

"Oh, yes, and that opal you are always fingering," he went on. "You think it is just a pretty keepsake, don't you? Your lucky charm. No, no, it is much more than that. That opal is more powerful than you could ever imagine. It is true you do not understand, Little Bird. Prepare yourself for the truth about your parents."

Gustave sat down and began to pour himself a fresh glass of wine as Rémy clasped her opal, her mind whirling. What was he talking about? Her parents? Gustave had never spoken of them before. Of course he hadn't, Gustave had no more idea who her parents were than she. Did he? What hideous game was he playing?

Gustave sighed heavily. "Your parents were cursed, Rémy, as I, too, am cursed. To lift the curse we must return the diamond. The diamond that you . . ."

A noise outside the caravan door startled Gustave. It was the sound of Claudette's voice, purposefully raised so that Gustave and Rémy would hear her.

"You cannot enter!" she was saying. "You have no right!"

"I am looking for a thief, madam — and I am the police," came a male voice. "I have every right."

"It's the policeman," Rémy hissed as Claudette continued to protest, "the one I took the jewel from! *Mon Dieu* — what am I going to do?"

Gustave's face distorted into fury once again. "Whatever it is, Little Bird, you had better be quick!"

Rémy looked around, panic-stricken. "The window. I'll escape through the window," she said, running toward it.

Gustave grabbed her arm, jolting her to a standstill, and thrust his face into hers. "Who knows how many policemen you have brought to my circus. We could be surrounded."

Rémy was unable to halt the frightened sob that left her lips as Gustave threw her to the other side of the room. But instead of advancing on her, he crouched and began to scrabble at the edge of the carpet, lifting a section of it to reveal a small trapdoor hidden in the caravan's floor.

"This is your only possible route of escape, Little Bird." Gustave said.

"Stand aside," Thaddeus's voice thundered outside, "or I will arrest you for obstructing the work of an officer going about his duties!"

Chapter 5

TAKING FLIGHT

"*W*hat are you waiting for?" Gustave hissed, his hand on the open trapdoor.

Rémy looked at the door to the caravan. Thaddeus Rec was still banging on it, so hard she thought the hinges might pop. For a second she thought about throwing herself on his mercy — after all, he'd tried to catch her when she fell, so he was surely a good man at heart. But she abandoned that idea almost immediately. He'd probably never known a day of hardship in his life. What sympathy could a policeman have for a circus rat like her?

"The curse," she whispered to Gustave. "You said there was a curse. What is it? How —"

He rattled the trapdoor with his fist. "Get it back, Little Bird. Bring the Ocean to me, and then I will explain everything. But you must get it back."

"What if I can't?" she whispered. "What if —"

"If you cannot?" Gustave sucked air through his teeth. "Then do not bother to return at all. Now, go."

What else could she do but obey? Rémy jumped through the trapdoor, landing on the grass below, and immediately dropped into a crouch as Gustave closed the opening over her head. She heard him slide the carpet back into place before slowly making his way to the caravan door, unlocking it and letting the policeman in. Once the door was closed, the men began to talk, but their voices were too muffled for her to make out what they were saying.

She had to get away. Rémy checked that the coast was clear and then scrambled out from under the caravan. The lights of the circus were dwindling as it closed for the night, but Claudette was waiting for her in the shadows, clutching a drawstring bag in her hands. She pulled Rémy to a safe distance and thrust the bag toward her.

"Clothes," Claudette whispered, "and the little money I have saved. Go. Get away from here, as fast as you can. And be safe."

Rémy held on to her friend, needles of fear stabbing at her heart. "I don't know where to go," she said. "I don't know what to do!"

Claudette pulled away and looked Rémy in the eye. "You are strong, Rémy, and clever. Keep to the poor streets — the places where the police do not go unless they have to."

Rémy felt her eyes filling with tears. "I don't know when I will see you again. I don't know —"

"Rémy," the fortune-teller whispered. "Listen to me. You will find that diamond and come back to me. I know it. You can do it. Now go, before Gustave throws that policeman out!"

Rémy took the bag and stumbled away, ducking from shadow to shadow as she made her way out of the circus field. At the roadside, she stopped and turned back to catch one last glimpse of Claudette, who stood motionless as stone, watching her. Rémy felt the tears run down her face, and wiped them away, angrily. She'd got herself into this mess, so there was no point feeling sorry for herself. Rémy turned her back on Le Cirque de la Lune — on the only home she had ever known — and plunged into the dark streets of London's East End.

* * *

"Apologies for not answering the door sooner. I have trouble with my leg, you see," said the circus owner, as he patted his thigh and limped slowly toward his chair.

"I heard voices," Thaddeus said, facing the enormously fat man who had introduced himself as Gustave. "In here, just now before I came in."

The man looked around and shrugged. "My singing, perhaps? As you see, there is no one here but me." He smiled, revealing his few remaining teeth, but the expression did not reach his eyes. "Except you, of course."

Thaddeus followed his gaze. The caravan was small and cramped, and he couldn't imagine anyone choosing to live in such a hovel. But then, Thaddeus knew, it was a lucky man who was able to choose how he lived.

"You have a performer here. A high wire act called Little Bird."

The circus master grinned again. "Ah, yes. Have you seen her? She is a wonder." He looked Thaddeus up and down, slyly. "She is pretty, too, no? Ah, but alas — she is not for sale."

Thaddeus blinked, and then frowned. This man made his skin crawl. "Where is she?"

The man sighed heavily, and then pulled out a

pocket watch. He made a show of flipping it open and checking the time before looking surprised.

"She has only been off the trapeze for . . . what? *Cinq* minutes? She is probably getting changed."

"You haven't seen her, then?"

The man shook his head. His lank hair remained still, slicked against his scalp. *"Non."*

"Do you know where she might be?"

The circus owner showed his teeth again. "Ah, well, she is slippery, that one. A good girl, really — but slippery. Wild." He shook with faint laughter. "It is why she is 'Little Bird,' yes? Because she is little, and . . . she flutters, here and there."

"What's her real name?"

The man frowned, as if Thaddeus had asked him a riddle. "Her real name? . . . She is Little Bird."

"No," Thaddeus said, impatiently. "Not her stage name. Her real name. What do you call her, when she is not performing?"

"Ah, I think I see what you mean." Gustave paused, a pained expression on his face as if he were trying hard to remember something long forgotten. "Moineau," the man said eventually.

"And her surname?" Thaddeus barked, becoming increasingly frustrated.

"Her surname . . . let me see . . ." Gustave hesitated again, letting out a long sigh. "Volant. Yes, Moineau Volant."

Thaddeus nodded, taking out his notepad and writing down the name. He asked Gustave to spell it for him, careful to make sure he got it right. Moineau Volant. Not Rémy Brunel.

"And the other circus performers would confirm that, would they?" he asked, looking up into the man's chubby, pale face. "If I asked them for her real name?"

"We all call her Little Bird, *monsieur*. I know not whether she has told others her 'real name' as you call it. If she has, then that will be the name they give you."

The policeman put away his notepad and pencil. "Yes," he said, thoughtfully. "Yes, I'm sure it will be."

* * *

The streets were slick with rain and Rémy did not like to think what else. Her silver slippers were soon soaked through and blackened by the grime that oozed over every cobble and encrusted the rough paving of the alleyways. She had to get rid of her circus costume. In these dark streets, it was beginning to attract attention. She might as well have shouted "I am a stranger and alone — come and get me."

She dodged into a dark hollow of moldering brick, crouching to open the bag that Claudette had given her. She found her favorite black shirt and belt, a pair of leggings and her trusty boots. There was also a thick cloak that Rémy recognized as belonging to her friend. Oh, how she loved her dear Claudette.

Pulling on the shirt, Rémy wriggled awkwardly out of the leotard. She hesitated for a moment, taking one last look at her dazzling costume, before using the fabric to scrub her face clean of the lingering grease-paint. As she stared at the smudge of mingled colors on the yellow satin, she wondered whether she would ever again perform as Little Bird. How would she survive without the circus? Of course, she had dreamed for so long of escaping it, of leaving that life behind. Yet, in those dreams, she had always had Claudette and Amélie by her side. Now she was cast adrift on an unknown ocean, without her friends, and she didn't know when, or even if, she would see them again.

Shaking her head clear, Rémy pulled on her leggings and then her cloak. She looked up at the ribbon of night sky, only just visible between the roofs over her head. It was late, and she was suddenly deathly tired. Around her, sounds were muted. There was only the odd burst of music rising through the open door of an all-night public house, and occasionally the hollow laughter of a drunken woman. She looked around the little alcove she had found and realized it was probably as safe a place as she would find to sleep tonight.

Wrapping her cloak more firmly around herself, Rémy sank to the ground and curled up with her head resting on her knees, the drawstring handle of her bag looped around one wrist. The wall was damp and uncomfortable against her back, and the cold bit at her despite Claudette's cloak. But eventually she slept, her dreams unhappy.

She was roused some time later by a slight tickle. It felt as if someone were brushing a feather against her arm. Her immediate thought was rats, and she shifted slightly, unafraid and too deeply asleep to stir properly. The feeling went away for a few minutes, and then came back with a vengeance. It wasn't a tickle, it was something tugging, something . . .

Rémy snapped awake properly as the drawstring of her bag gave beneath the knife sawing at it. She was on her feet in a second, but it was too late. The thief — a small, scrawny boy — had fled, his prize held tight in his arms.

"Hey!" she shouted at the cutpurse as he vanished down the alley. "Stop! You little —"

Rémy gave chase, dashing out into the gray, weak light of morning. It had begun to rain again. Icy drips of water slid down Rémy's neck, and she pulled the hood of her cloak up around her ears.

Rounding the corner after the boy, she found herself in a busier street. There were knots of people everywhere, huddled, crouching in corners or muttering together beside the crumbling brick walls. Pungent smoke — from the houses of those lucky enough to have a few lumps of coal, as well as from decrepit old pipes — hung in wraiths around their heads. The poisonous air was full of the sound of coughs and wails, shouts and the occasional scream, always cut short. Children skittered past her legs, as fast as rats and just as scrawny. The place reeked of hunger and decay, and there was desperation everywhere. Rémy knew poverty from France. It was a fearful disease and there was no cure, not in streets as poor as these.

She dodged and wove through the throngs of people, her boots echoing along the narrow alley walls. No one took any notice of her cries, or even turned to look at the fleeing boy, clutching her bag as his bony legs carried him along. He kept looking over his shoulder to see if Rémy had given up yet, but she was determined and, despite Gustave's tight-fistedness, still better fed than an East End street urchin. Besides, the bag and its contents were now all she had in the world. She wasn't going to let them go without a fight.

The thief ducked into an even narrower alley, and then immediately darted right, into another so narrow that two men would struggle to walk abreast. Rémy was quick, though, and followed easily. She could see that the boy was tiring, the distance between them lessening with every step.

"I'm not going to give up," she shouted after him. "So you might as well drop the bag!"

The boy didn't answer. He disappeared from sight instead. Rémy skidded to a stop where she'd last seen him, looking around, perplexed. Then, over the noise of rain and despair, she heard a faint metal clang. Looking up, she saw him shimmying up an old, rusting pipe, heading for the rooftops.

Rémy didn't hesitate. The pipe was fragile, but she was quick and nimble and the walls were so close together that she knew she could easily brace herself if necessary. She was quieter than the boy, too, so when she appeared on the roof beside him, he started.

"Not so fast," she snapped, as the wheezing child tried to scramble away. She pinned him by the shoulder, holding him still with one hand and ripping her bag from his grip with the other.

"Bleedin' 'eck!" The boy whimpered, looking back toward the roof's edge. "Where in 'ell d'you learn to climb like that?"

Rémy put the bag behind her out of his reach, but didn't let him go. "A good lesson to learn, rat. 'Never judge a book by its cover,' I believe you say here. Strangers might be out of place, but that does not make them helpless."

They were both breathing hard, and the boy didn't attempt to struggle from Rémy's grip. He seemed to have accepted that he'd been beaten, and his eyes closed as he caught his breath. Rémy thought he was probably about ten years old, but he was so thin and malnourished he looked younger. His face, lined with dirt, looked gaunt, his eyes dark hollows.

"Sorry," he said eventually. "Just 'ungry, y'see. 'Aven't 'ad a bite today. Not likely to, neither. Didn't 'ave one yesterday, come to think of it. And you looked like you could spare a bit."

"Well, you are wrong," Rémy told him, and then relented. After all, she knew no one here, or even where she was. Perhaps this was an opportunity to make a friend — or at least buy one for a while. She let him go and opened the bag, searching for the purse that contained the money Claudette had given her.

"I have not eaten either," she told the boy. "I bet you know somewhere we can get a meal for little money, yes?"

The boy blinked at her. "Eh?"

"I won't ask twice. I do not make a habit of buying meals for my enemies, so you'd better make yourself my friend before I change my mind."

He scrambled up with a quick grin. "We can go to The Grapes. It ain't far."

As Rémy stood up, she asked, "What is your name?"

"J," he said. "Friends call me J."

She nodded. "*D'accord*, J. Lead the way."

* * *

"Where'd you learn to speak English so proper, any-way?" J asked, an hour or so later, his mouth stuffed full of greasy bacon. They were sitting in the narrow, wood-paneled dining room of The Grapes. It was so close to the Thames that Rémy could smell the sewage stench of the river even though they had opted to sit inside, rather than on the shabby balcony that hung over the water.

She rested her chin on one hand and shrugged. "Claudette — a friend — taught me."

"Oh, yeah? Frenchie too, is she?"

"Yes."

"So where'd she learn it, then?"

Rémy frowned. It was a question that had never occurred to her before. Claudette always seemed to know something about everything. It was just the way she was. "I don't know."

J nodded, then carried on shoving food into his mouth, losing interest in his question in favor of the first proper meal he'd had in weeks.

"Where are your parents?" Rémy asked.

J shrugged. "Dunno. Never really 'ad any. There was me mum, once, but . . . she went."

"Where do you live, then?"

"Here an' there. Why?" he asked, suspiciously. "There ain't no more room for no one else, if that's what you're thinkin'."

Rémy shook her head. "I'm just passing through. Looking for someone."

"Oh? Who's that, then?"

"His name is Abernathy."

J's fork froze on its way to his mouth. He even stopped chewing for a moment. He didn't lift his chin, but looked up at her from beneath his brow. "What d'you want to find 'im for?"

Rémy shifted in her seat. "You know him? Is he really a lord?"

The boy snorted. "Yeah. Yeah, 'e's a lord, all right. Listen to the Sally Ann and you'd think 'e was a bleedin' saint."

Rémy frowned. "Sally Ann?"

J shook his head. "Don't you have 'em in France? The Salvation Army. They're the only ones'll feed you down 'ere if you ain't got nuffin'. Give you a bed for the night too, if you read a bit of the good book wiv 'em. Won't give you booze, though. Don't hold with it." J snickered through his food then looked back at Rémy, his expression suddenly serious. "You want to keep away from 'im, though. Abernathy, I mean. I reckon 'e's dodgy as a fish stall after four o' the clock."

She leaned forward. "Why? Why do you think that?"

J resumed shoveling food into his mouth, taking a breath to lift his now-empty pint glass. "Could murder another pint o' porter, I could."

Rémy shook her head. "Tell me about Lord Abernathy, then we'll see."

"What do you want to know about 'im for, any-way?" J asked evasively.

"He stole something. Something valuable. Something I want. Something the police think I already have."

J snorted. "The coppers? They're about as useful as a cold cup o' tea. They won't follow you down 'ere, and they won't do nuffin' about Abernathy, that's for sure."

"How do you know?"

"'E's got friends in 'igh places. He's a lord, ain't he? Stands to reason. And . . ." J trailed off, staring at his plate.

"And what? Come on, J. Tell me."

J shrugged. "People 'ave been going missing for months down 'ere," he said. "No one cares, cos it's just us, ain't it? But me mate, he went one night, and I got to thinking. Got to looking around a bit more, like. And I reckon . . . Well, I reckon it's 'im."

"Abernathy? You think he's kidnapping people?"

"Shh," J hissed, looking around to see if anyone had overheard. "Keep your voice down!"

"All right, all right," said Rémy, lowering her voice.

The boy fiddled with his glass for another moment, before he said, "I dunno. It's just a hunch. The Sally

Ann reckon 'e's all about building new 'omes for us poor folk. They say that's why 'e's bought up all the old mines. Improvin' our lives, they say. 'E's definitely got something going on down there in those tunnels. But I don't think he's buildin' bits o' 'omes. I reckon it's something else."

"What?"

J shrugged. "How should I know?"

"Have you told anyone?" Rémy asked.

J snorted again, but this time it was a sadder sound. "Who's goin' to listen to me?"

Rémy shrugged. "I am."

The boy eyed her. "Yeah, but you're like me, really, ain't you? I mean, besides being a foreigner an' all that."

"Where are these mines?" Rémy asked after a moment. "Can you take me there?"

J looked at her with the steady stare of someone speaking to an addled mind. "As if. You'd not catch me getting close to 'em. I'm not being caught. No, sir. Life's bad enough already." He banged his empty glass on the table. "I can take you to 'is house, though. So, what about that porter, eh? Fair's fair, ain't it?"

Chapter 6

SUSPICIONS AND ACCUSATIONS

*H*aving interviewed as many of the circus folk as he could find and searched around for clues, it was the early hours of the morning by the time Thaddeus returned to Scotland Yard. The old building glimmered in the fresh rain, and he was surprised to see that there were still lights on in the wing occupied by the detective division. His colleagues were not known for working late.

He felt eyes following him as he pushed through the wooden double doors and headed for his desk. There was a sudden hush, as if all conversations in the room had become unnecessary. Collins appeared from nowhere, looking surly.

"About time you showed up, boy. This place is in uproar because of you." Collins nodded over his shoulder to the shut door of Chief Inspector Glove's office. "He's out for blood."

Thaddeus nodded wearily as he dropped into his chair. He'd known as much, even without being told. "What is being done?" he asked Collins. "Have they questioned the guards? Do they have any more information about the girl?"

The other policeman crossed his arms. He opened his mouth to speak, too, but before Collins had a chance, the Chief Inspector's door opened and Glove appeared. His gaze fell upon Thaddeus immediately and darkened. Thaddeus quickly stood up again.

"Rec."

Thaddeus nodded toward his superior. "Chief Inspector."

Glove looked slowly around the room. The other detectives fell even quieter. The hush filled the room like a bubble ready to burst.

"So," Glove said, a question in his voice. "Did you find the suspect — this girl you went to apprehend at . . . the circus?"

"She —" Thaddeus shook his head. "She wasn't there, sir."

The Chief Inspector looked at him steadily. "She wasn't there."

"No, sir. Or at least — she was there." He looked at Collins for support. "Collins saw her, same as me. When we first arrived, she was in the middle of her act, sir. But after that . . . she vanished."

Glove turned his gaze on Collins. "And can you confirm that the girl you saw on the trapeze was the same girl at Lord Abernathy's side earlier this evening, Collins?"

There was a pause. Collins's cheeks reddened. Thaddeus felt the knot in his stomach tighten. "I . . . No, sir," said Collins. "No. I can't."

"Collins!" Thaddeus said. "But you saw —"

The other man shook his head, impatient. "What I saw, lad, was a circus girl on a wire. Her face was so covered in paint, even her mother would find it hard to recognize her! Secondly, how you think she stole the jewel and got back in time to be up there, doing her act, is beyond me. And thirdly —" Collins shrugged, looking at the Chief Inspector. "Does there need to be a thirdly, Chief?"

Glove raised one eyebrow. "Probably not. So how do you explain all this, young Rec?"

"But . . . but she disappeared straight after her act,"

Thaddeus stuttered. "No one would tell me where she was. And I swear, it was her, I know it."

"It's very convenient, isn't it?" said Glove. "You alone are convinced that the girl at the Tower is the same girl you saw at the circus. And now that girl has also vanished. And didn't I hear that you were hanging around the circus last night — looking for a buyer perhaps?"

Thaddeus shook his head, confused. What was happening here? "A buyer? Sir, I don't —"

"Well," continued the chief inspector, "it just so happens that you were the last one to be in possession of the Shah of Persia's diamond."

Thaddeus felt his blood freeze in his veins. "Sir? W-what are you suggesting?"

"Well, my boy, we only have your word for it that the diamond wasn't in your pocket when you started yelling blue murder. Don't we?" Glove began to pace, hands in his pockets. "You went running off after a lord and a girl, claiming one of them had nicked it, and ran straight out of the Tower. Of course, no one even contemplated stopping you. Then all of a sudden, you decided that the place to find this girl was the circus. The circus! Where every good man knows that every bad man finds his level. The perfect place, in fact, to fence a stolen jewel if, of course, you had one. Now don't you think that's all a little odd, boys, a little . . . convenient, perhaps?"

There was a murmur of assent among the gathered detectives. Thaddeus cast a fevered look around their familiar faces and suddenly felt as if he were staring at strangers.

"Sir," he began hoarsely. "Sir, you can't really believe that of me. This is — sir, this is me!"

Glove stopped pacing and stood before Thaddeus. He looked the younger man up and down once before nodding heavily.

"Yes. Yes, it is you, Rec. And I'm sorry to say that I was fool enough to believe that a leopard could change his spots. Now, people may say that it's admirable — the son of thieves wanting to dedicate his life to the police. I thought so, too, at the time. It's why I gave you a chance, Rec. I thought you might be a good example to others." Glove held up his hand to silence the other detectives who had begun to mutter upon hearing this hint about Thaddeus's past. "But I went too far, didn't I? Gave you free reign, let you inside, so to speak. Trusted you. Where were you born, Rec?"

Thaddeus blinked. "W-Whitechapel Road, sir."

"Oh, yes, that's right. Remind me which house on Whitechapel Road, Rec."

Thaddeus felt his cheeks burning hot as his vision blurred. The murmuring started again as he shook his head and whispered, "Not in a house, sir. On the street. I was born . . . on the street."

"Ah, yes," said Glove, his eyes gleaming. "I remember now."

Thaddeus forced himself to straighten up and raise his head, despite his shame. "It doesn't matter where I came from, sir, and you know it. I'm a good copper."

The chief inspector crossed his arms. "Is that so? And what, as a good copper, do you suggest we do now then, Rec?"

"I think we should talk to Lord Abernathy. He was with the girl at the Tower. He might know —"

Glove made a sound of disgust deep in his throat. "So, now you're proposing to question a lord of the realm, are you, Rec? And Lord Abernathy at that — a pillar of respectable society. You? And what makes you think you have the right to do that? What makes you think you have the right to cast doubt on a nobleman?"

Thaddeus frowned. "No — not doubt, sir. But he may know something. Surely it would help?"

"I don't see how. No, Rec, we'll not find the culprit among the good society of London. We'll have to look at the lower orders for that." Glove paused, looking significantly at Thaddeus. "Which brings us back to you, doesn't it, Rec? Why did you stay at the circus, after Collins here had realized it was a wild goose chase?"

Thaddeus shut his eyes briefly. "I wanted to find out more about the girl — the trapeze performer."

"And why did you want to do that?"

"Because I thought there was still a chance that it was the same girl who was at the Tower when the jewel went missing, sir."

"And what did you find out, then? On this urgent and, if I may say so, probably pointless mission?"

With a shaking hand, Thaddeus took out his note-book and opened it to the page that he'd scrawled on earlier. "I found out her real name, sir. I think we might be able to trace her. Find out if she's been in trouble for a similar crime before. Her real name is — Moineau Volant."

Glove froze for a second, frowning. Then he burst into laughter. Thaddeus watched him, confused and not a little afraid.

"Sir?" he asked. "What's — what's so funny?"

"That's her name, is it, Rec? Moineau Volant?"

"Yes, sir — several of the circus folk confirmed it."

Glove shook his head, his laughter still ringing in Thaddeus's ears. "It's not a name, Rec — or at least, it's not a real one. But then, what should I expect? That a boy born in the sewer would know a refined language like French?" The chief inspector snatched the notepad from his hand, glancing at it before holding it up for all to see. "Moineau Volant, indeed. It means 'Flying Sparrow,' Rec. Flying Sparrow."

Flying Sparrow. A second ticked by, empty and cold, and then — *Yes*, thought Thaddeus, as realization washed over him, followed by dread. *Yes. A little bird, indeed, and one who flies through the air every night.*

"So, Rec — your sparrow has flown away and, with it, your suspect. Which brings me back to thinking about how the diamond vanished, and who it was with when it did — you."

Thaddeus stared at his superior officer, feeling everything spinning out of his control. All his colleagues were looking at him, their eyes full of suspicion and disdain. How could they think he took the stone? How could they? More importantly, how could he prove that he didn't without finding the person who had?

"Chief Inspector, I suggest that you search the circus. It's there, sir. It must be! You'll have to move quickly, before they pack up and disappear."

"And what should I do with you in the meantime, Rec? Let you go free? Let you 'help' us find it? Let you wriggle your way out by pinning the theft on someone else?"

For a second, Thaddeus was speechless. Could they really be accusing him of this crime? "Sir," he said. "I have never stolen a thing in my life. You know I wouldn't do this." Glove's face remained stony. He looked at Collins, instead. "Collins, you know me. You know I wouldn't!"

Collins shook his head and looked away. "Sorry, son," he said, quietly. "But I don't know anything."

"Take him away, Collins," said the Chief Inspector. "Thaddeus Rec, you are under arrest for the theft of the Darya-ye Noor —"

"Wait!" Thaddeus shouted desperately, "No, you cannot possibly believe that I —"

"Put him in one of the cells downstairs overnight, Collins," Glove continued, ignoring Thaddeus. "We'll all get some rest and question him properly in the morning. He might be more cooperative then."

"No," shouted Thaddeus again, "No, wait, I . . ."

"Come on, boy," said Collins calmly, placing a hand on Thaddeus's arm. "Come quietly now. You know the drill. If you're innocent you've got nothing to worry about, have you? Don't make things worse for yourself, eh? There's a good lad."

Rec stared at the older policeman for a moment. He felt as if all the stuffing had been knocked out of him. He loved being a policeman. The detective division had become his life, his whole purpose. And now they had turned on him. All of them. What was the point, if they didn't believe him now? His shoulders dropped and he nodded at Collins. Together, they walked out of the room, every pair of eyes following their progress.

They were in the cold corridor that led to the cells when Collins stopped.

"Hit me," he whispered.

Thaddeus stared at him. "What?"

"Come on, boy! Hit me and run! We haven't got much time!"

"But you said —"

"Aye, I knows what I said. That was for them, weren't it? Now I'm saying to you, clout me one and scarper before they know what's happening. You won't get a fair deal in here — a copper, gone bad, and one born to the streets at that? They'll have your guts for garters. You didn't take it, lad, I know that. You don't have a bad bone in you. But in here, you'll never prove it. So come on — hit me!"

Thaddeus shook his head. "I can't!"

Collins grabbed him by the shoulders and shook him hard. "For God's sake! They'll hang you out to dry unless we can prove you didn't do it, Thaddeus! And not one of them will bother even trying. They've got their man, as far as they're concerned. Don't you understand? Naught you can do from inside a cell. Hit me, boy! Quick, before someone comes!"

Behind them, there came the sound of raised voices — the rest of the division were preparing to head home. He looked Collins in the eye. The older man nodded.

"Come on, lad," he said, softly. "You can do it."

"I can't," Thaddeus said, biting his lip. "Collins, you're just going to have to take me to the cells. I just can't."

The older man shook his head. He opened his mouth to speak again, but whatever he was about to say was interrupted. The door at the other end of the corridor — the one that led to fresh air and freedom — banged open, forced back on its hinges so violently that it struck the wall, sending a plume of paint and plaster into the air. Through it strode a tall, bald man who seemed to be spreading smoke in his wake. He wore no hat, and the pale skin of his head shone faintly in the sickly light of the hallway. His black wool tailcoat was covered with dust, which somehow lent him a ghostly air, and the heels of his dirty boots clicked sharply on the worn wooden floor.

"Stand aside, sir," shouted the newcomer at Collins. "Unhand the boy!"

Collins raised his hands, but before he could say anything, the stranger had pulled something from inside his coat and took aim at the policeman. In shape it vaguely resembled a pistol, but there the similarity ended. It was like no gun Thaddeus had ever seen. It was the size of a loaf of bread, and silver, with a thin central column that attached a bulbous handle to a chamber of purple liquid at one end and a small dish-like muzzle at the other. This was the end that the man was pointing at the terrified Collins.

"Wait," Thaddeus exclaimed as the man prepared to fire. "Wait, don't —"

Behind him, the door at the other end of the corridor opened as the rest of the detective division headed for home, led by a rosy-cheeked and triumphant Chief Inspector Glove.

"You, there!" the Chief Inspector shouted, stopping dead when he saw the scene unfolding in front of him. "What the devil are you doing?"

The stranger fired. His peculiar pistol shot a column of compressed purple air straight at Collins's face. The policeman's surprised eyes clouded over immediately, and he slumped against the wall before sliding to the floor in a heap. The intruder then turned the weapon on Glove, who uttered an unceremonious yell and dived for the floor, the rest of the detectives following suit.

The stranger grabbed Thaddeus's arm. "Come on," he urged, pulling him toward the door.

Chapter 7

THE TRUTH IN
THE LIE

"Get off me!" Thaddeus struggled, trying to free himself from the man's grasp, which was surprisingly strong. "Who are you? Leave me alone!"

The intruder ignored Thaddeus's protests and dragged him toward the exit as Glove and his men got back to their feet. Thaddeus was propelled through the door and stumbled down the wet steps outside, faltering on the cobbles as the stranger forced him onward.

"Boy, if you don't run now, we'll both be caught."

"Then let us be caught! You shot Collins! He was trying to help me!"

"And so am I! It was only sleeping gas, for God's sake! Come on, Thaddeus — run!"

Something in the man's voice made Thaddeus look up, meeting the stranger's eyes. They were shaded by the night and his ridiculously bushy eyebrows, but still Rec caught a distinctive flash of blue in their depths. He started.

"Professor?"

"Of course it's me. Who did you expect, the Queen of Sheba? Now run, damn you!"

The Professor took off, out of Scotland Yard and into the flickering gaslight. Thaddeus kept close on his heels, hearing the shouts and sharp tin whistles of the police behind them. It seemed as if the whole of the Yard had joined the chase. The Professor ducked down one street that was swathed in darkness and then turned a sharp right and ran straight down another.

"Professor," Thaddeus managed to say, between heaving breaths. "Professor, you're leading us straight toward High Holborn. There will be people every-where!"

"Exactly," the disguised professor called back over his shoulder, without a pause. "Safety in numbers, boy! Keep close, now!"

The street they were on suddenly opened out into a wider thoroughfare, which even at this early hour was busy with carriages. The Professor didn't cross the road, as Thaddeus had expected, but instead charged toward a hansom cab parked at the corner of the British Museum. He opened the door, shouting something to the driver before looking back toward Thaddeus.

"Come on! Hurry!"

Thaddeus vaulted up the cab's step and into its interior, crashing against the soft seat as his friend jumped in behind him. The Professor raised his fist and hammered once against the wooden panel beside Thaddeus. The cab took off at once, sliding smoothly into the channel of anonymous horse-drawn traffic streaming down the road.

"Ahh!" exclaimed the Professor, leaning back against the seat, out of breath. "That was a close one, eh?"

Thaddeus shook his head, also breathing hard. "You're mad. Completely, totally mad! And what have you done to yourself?"

The Professor laughed, leaning forward and running a hand over the blank canvas of his shiny head. "Do you like it? I think it's rather fetching, myself."

Thaddeus reached out and hesitantly poked at the pale skin. It was slightly spongy to the touch. "That's horrible! And those eyebrows! That nose! You look . . . awful!"

The Professor leaned back and sighed. "Ah well, never mind, I'll remove it as soon as we get to the workshop. It did the trick though, didn't it? Even you failed to recognize me. And if I hadn't done what I did, you'd be languishing in a cell right now."

Thaddeus looked out of the window, watching the night streets of London pass by, lit by the occasional tame halo of gaslight. He suddenly felt very, very tired. The motion of the cab rocked him from side to side as it rattled over the cobbles, moving east. He slipped into a doze and didn't wake until the driver pulled the horse to a standstill. Thaddeus blinked sleepily as the Professor leaned over and poked him with a bony finger.

"Come on, then, Thaddeus Rec," he said. "Let's get inside, eh?"

Thaddeus stumbled from the cab, realizing that they were at Limehouse Basin, which meant they were going to the Professor's workshop. The dock was already busy, even though dawn had yet to color the sky above the grimy wharves. Men shouted as they heaved goods onto the waiting boats that bobbed about in the oily, choppy water of the Thames. He nodded to a couple that he recognized as they skirted the edge of the Basin, faces he knew from his occasional drinks in The Grapes public house, just a few minutes' walk away.

They slipped down one of the alleyways behind Oliver's Wharf. The Professor glanced about him before pulling a heavy bunch of keys from his pocket and slotting one into the lock of an unimportant-looking door. He pushed it open and disappeared into darkness. Thaddeus waited until he heard the sound of a match struck and the faint light of a candle lit his way. Then he followed the Professor, stepping inside and closing the door behind him.

"Excuse me for a few moments, won't you?" called the Professor, disappearing into his private study at the other end of the room. "Just going to remove this face you so heartily disapprove of."

Rec nodded absently as he shut the study door. He had been here a hundred times and had spent hours tinkering with the objects gathered about him, but he still found himself taking an extra breath when he entered the workshop. For one thing, it was just so huge. It took up the whole lower floor of the Wharf, and at some point the Professor had knocked through all the walls save the supporting ones, leaving the space open. Into the resulting cavern was crammed every manner of wonderful, inexplicable mechanical gadgetry, creating a merry mess that overflowed the many workbenches and shelves and spilled onto the floor in piles of cogs, springs, levers, and other bits and pieces.

One bench was dedicated to the workings of clocks, because the Professor was convinced that there was a way to make a pocket watch that would communicate with another watch of the same design, worn by a different person. He thought it would be possible to send messages from one to the other by means of a small electrical current, and so to experiment he had taken hundreds of them apart and wired them all up in different ways. Their collective ticking produced a whirring hum that filled Thaddeus's ears like a swarm of bees as he passed.

Then there was the rocket pack. If Thaddeus was honest, this was the invention that he was most excited about. He kept trying to persuade the Professor to let him test it out, but the answer was always "It's not ready yet."

The idea was to create a steam-powered engine small enough for a man to carry on his back. The Professor was currently working on the idea that if he built a cylinder that produced a vacuum at one end and propulsion at the other, the force and motion

could lift a grown man off the ground. It was a dangerous enterprise — the boiling steam alone could kill a
man — but Thaddeus couldn't wait to try it. Imagine
being able to walk in the air — to fly like a bird. Of
course, the Professor hadn't quite worked out how to
steer the thing yet, but Thaddeus had faith that it was
only a matter of time.

The young detective dropped into a chair in front
of the bench that seemed to hold the secrets of the
Professor's latest weapon — the gas pistol he had
used so effectively back at Scotland Yard. Thaddeus
had never seen it before. He set about trying to understand how it worked while he waited for his friend to
return.

"How did you know?" Thaddeus asked, once the
Professor had changed out of his disguise. The trans-
formation was remarkable — no one would have
known that the man who had burst into the police
station was the same man who bustled about the place
now. The bald head was gone, replaced by a flash of
fine white hair, and the bushy eyebrows and hooked
nose had vanished, too. It was impossible to pinpoint
the Professor's age — the eyes said late thirties, but
the hair suggested he was much older. Thaddeus had
never had the courage to ask.

"How did I know what?"

"About what was happening at the station. I mean, you just turned up, out of nowhere."

The Professor was busy taking apart the weapon he had used on Collins, cleaning it down and refilling the chamber of purple liquid from a heated glass vial that had been steaming gently over a Bunsen burner.

"I had been listening in, dear boy," he said. "To begin with, I thought that man Glove was being merely unpleasant. Then I realized he was actually a complete fool. And a dangerous one at that, I'll warrant."

Thaddeus frowned. "Listening in? Whatever do you mean?"

The Professor carefully replaced the glass vial on its stand before going to Thaddeus's coat, which he had folded across the empty chair beside him. The Professor shook it out, his hand reaching for the bottom seam, where the lining met the outer wool. He probed about for a bit, and then took a sharp knife from the workbench and quickly slit it open.

"Professor!" Thaddeus said in dismay, "that's my only coat!"

"Please don't fuss, Rec," said the older man. "It's easily repaired. Have you never heard of a needle and thread? Aha, there!"

The Professor pulled a small metal object — or rather, a collection of small metal objects — from Thaddeus's coat. Among the tangle of parts, Thaddeus could see several tiny cogs, a miniature gauge, and some metal piping, as well as what looked like a small cylinder at the center, covered in a very thin layer of foil. Attached to the gauge was a small, red jewel that looked to Thaddeus like garnet. The object was fascinating and beautiful.

"What is it?" he asked, taking the device from the Professor's hands and turning it over, careful not to break any of the fragile parts.

"Well, in part it is a very small friction engine," said the Professor. "The smallest I've ever built — in fact, I'll wager it is the smallest anyone has ever built. It's started by external movement. That's why I put it at the bottom of your coat. When you put the garment on and begin to walk, the engine starts up."

"I don't understand," Thaddeus said. "You said you were listening? To what happened at the station?"

"Ah, yes," said the Professor. "Well you see, that's the truly genius bit of this device. Once the thing's warmed up and ticking over nicely, it can send a signal."

"A signal?"

"Yes. It's a recording, really. It works like Mr.

Edison's phonograph — the one that caused all the fuss last year. But unlike him, I got it working properly. The key is the tin foil, you know! He was using wax, which was simply foolish. You see here —" he pointed to the cylinder at the center of the device. "When the engine starts, the stylus begins to make little indentations in the foil that, when played back at a faster rate, will recreate the sounds it is picking up. It can only store two or three minutes at a time, so once it is full it uses its friction energy to transmit to a larger unit. The one in question is on the roof of Scotland Yard, incidentally. I put it there a few months back — and that relays to this . . ."

In full flow now, the Professor pointed expansively to a large phonograph that stood on another workbench. It had been augmented with an extra speaker horn and a tower of thin metal filaments that disappeared into the ceiling.

"The same patterns that were recorded at your end are etched onto another, larger cylinder at this end, you see," the Professor continued to an astonished Thaddeus. "I have it set to play back immediately and continuously, as soon as the friction engine is activated. Of course, there's a little delay. That's why I was almost too late. It's lucky you're a ditherer by nature, my boy!"

Thaddeus was speechless for a few moments, looking between the tiny device that had been hidden in his coat and the gramophone.

"It's amazing," he said eventually. "Simply amazing."

"Yes, it is rather, isn't it?"

"You're a genius."

The Professor sniffed happily. "Oh well, Thaddeus, genius is as genius does, you know."

Then something else occurred to Thaddeus. He frowned. "Were you spying on me?"

The older man looked genuinely shocked. "What? Of course not!"

"But you put this in my coat," Thaddeus pointed out. "How long has it been there? What were you hoping to hear? Or were you using me to get inside the police station? Is that what this is all about?"

The Professor placed a hand on his arm. "Thaddeus, Thaddeus," he soothed. "It wasn't anything of the kind. I merely wanted to be able to test the machine, that's all. It's far from perfect yet."

"Well, why didn't you just ask me to test it for you? You know I always try to help with your experiments if I can."

The Professor sighed. "What time did you get home last night?"

"Well, I haven't actually been home yet."

"And the night before?"

"Err . . ."

"And the night before that?" The Professor held up a hand before he could reply. "My dear boy, you are never anywhere but at work. You are always at Scotland Yard or about police business. And I knew you would never agree to allow me to listen into the police station. But who else could I ask? So . . . there we are."

Thaddeus sighed. "You shouldn't have done it, you know."

"Ah, but think of the benefits!" the Professor exclaimed gleefully. "Think of the criminal organizations we could take down! No one could hide from the law!"

Thaddeus had to smile at the Professor's enthusiasm, though his humor soon turned cold. "I don't think I'll ever be catching criminals again," he said, quietly. "I'm a wanted man myself now."

The Professor patted his shoulder again. "Don't you worry about that. Now, I don't think I caught everything clearly with my friction machine. Tell me all about it — start from the beginning."

And so Thaddeus did. He left nothing out, from the night at the circus just three days ago when he had seen, and tried to save, the girl they called Little Bird, right up until when the Professor had burst through the doors of Scotland Yard just an hour or so ago. In the retelling of it all, the events of the past three days seemed surreal and unbelievable even to Thaddeus, but the Professor listened patiently, nodding here and there.

"Well," he said, when the story was done. "This is a curious matter and no mistake. First things first — you'd better give me those night glasses. I'll see if I can get them working." Thaddeus dug them out of his coat pocket and handed them over as the Professor went on, "What do you plan to do next?"

Thaddeus shrugged. "What can I do, except try to find the real thief? She's out there somewhere. I just have to find her."

The Professor nodded, a thoughtful frown on his face. "And you are sure? That she is the thief?"

"Who else could it have been?"

His friend raised his shoulders slightly in an elegant shrug. "Things are not always as they seem, Thaddeus. You would do well to remember that."

Thaddeus pulled out his pocket watch and looked at the time. It was just touching five o'clock in the morning. He stood up, taking hold of his now even more tattered coat. "Well," he said, "in this case, Professor, I know exactly how things are. And I intend to put them right before I end up paying for a crime I did not commit."

"Where are you going?"

"To interrupt Lord Abernathy's breakfast. I've got to start somewhere, haven't I?"

Chapter 8

AN UNEXPECTED MEETING

"Well, look on the bright side," J whispered hoarsely, reaching up to pull a branch out of Rémy's way. "It ain't raining. Right?"

Rémy pushed forward through the undergrowth. J was right, the interminable rain had paused for a little while, but the bushes and grass around them were still soaking wet and the air was damp and clinging.

"It will be getting light soon," she said quietly, glancing at the sky.

"Tsk, don't you worry about that," J told her dismissively. "There's still plenty o' dark in the sky. Anyway, this is just a look-see, right? You ain't breaking in or nuffin'. Yet. Are yer?"

Rémy ignored him, pushing forward through yet another dripping bush. The night was always darkest before the dawn, they said, but it wasn't the dark that bothered her — it was the cold. She pulled Claudette's cloak more tightly about her shoulders and tried to ignore how icy her toes had become.

They were standing just inside the high brick wall of Lord Abernathy's house at Beauvoir Square, about a third of a mile west of Whitechapel. It was large and square, built of pale yellow London brick that glowed faintly in the dim light, and set in about an acre of grounds. At the other end of the estate, against the far reach of the wall, was a set of outbuildings, probably for the gardener's use.

"It is still not as big as I would have expected," she muttered, to herself as much as anyone else. "Not for a lord."

"Ah, well, this ain't 'is main place, is it? 'E's got a big place up north, so people say. An estate," J said significantly. "Scotland, I fink. Stands to reason, don' it? 'Is name sounds like a Scot, don' yer fink?"

Rémy didn't answer — she was too busy counting the windows that she could see. There were sixteen, and they were all closed fast and darkened. It didn't seem as if the lord was awake yet. She guessed that his servants would be, though. It was fast approaching the crowing hour now and they'd be scuttling around in the windowless basement, stoking the fires to warm the house ready for when His Lordship rose.

"I want to get closer," she said.

"All righ', if you must, but just watch yerself. I ain't coming to rescue yer if you get caught. *Oi!*" he added anxiously, as she kicked her boots off. "What'cha doin'? You ain't planning to shimmy your way up no more drainpipes, are ya?"

Rémy danced from one bare foot to the other, trying to get some feeling back into them. She nodded to the gravel path that ran around the edge of the house and cut through the neatly-manicured lawn. "Less noise this way," she said.

"Oh," said J, with a nod. "Well, when you put it like that . . ."

Rémy glanced at him. J's legs were barely covered by the tattered rags that stood for his trousers, and he was shivering in the cold morning air. She pulled off her cloak and pushed it toward him.

"Put it on," she ordered shortly. "Stay here. I will not be long."

"Cor!" J said, his eyes as big as the large round pennies he rarely saw. "Fanks!"

Rémy left him cocooning himself in the warm material and pushed her way out of the undergrowth, stepping onto the close-cut grass. She moved quickly, avoiding the gravel paths to muffle her progress. She had to work out where the Darya-ye Noor was likely being hidden. Abernathy would keep it close, she guessed, but nowhere obvious — probably his study. He might have a strongbox, or perhaps, if she was fortunate, just a locked drawer. Although her legendary luck had been out of sorts ever since she reached England, she reminded herself, as her bare feet slid into a puddle left from the last downpour.

Rémy reached the wall of the house and looked up. There were four floors, each with four windows. A bit grand for one person, even if he was a lord. Rémy thought back to Gustave's pronouncement that Abernathy was nothing of the kind. She wondered why he had said that — J had seemed convinced that he was. Rémy sighed to herself. It was funny; she'd spent her life at the circus trying to avoid spending time with Gustave, but now there were many things she'd like to ask him. She wondered if she'd ever get the chance.

Shaking her head, Rémy forced herself to concentrate. She had to see inside. If she could understand the layout of the house, it might give her a clue as to where Abernathy was hiding the stone. Rémy glanced back toward the bush where J was hiding. The boy would be horrified if he knew what she was contemplating, but she had no choice.

Placing her hands against the rough stone, Rémy looked up. There were plenty of handholds if you were brave enough. She took a deep breath. Then she began to climb.

She made it as far as the second floor and was balancing on a narrow brick window ledge when she heard a sound that chilled her blood. It was a dog barking — no, not one, not even two — it was the baleful sound of a whole pack. It was hard to pinpoint where they were, but the noise was getting louder by the second. Rémy looked over to the bush where she'd left J and saw that he'd scrambled out of his hiding place and was now standing on the lawn, frantically trying to attract her attention. On finally catching her eye, he shouted something she couldn't hear and then pointed to the other end of the grounds, around the corner of Abernathy's house, back toward the outbuildings she'd noticed earlier. He looked terrified.

A second later, the dogs appeared. There were five of them — huge and black, with slavering jaws opened wide to display their massive teeth. J turned to run, but there was no way he'd make it back to the wall in time. Rémy looked up — she could climb higher and get to the roof — there was no reason to think that the servants knew there was more than one intruder. She could sit up there all day if she had to and slip out once they'd locked the dogs away again.

But that would mean leaving J to his fate. She looked down again, seeing the scrawny little figure slipping and sliding over the wet grass as the dogs grew closer. Of course she couldn't leave him. He was just a child, and she was the only reason he was here at all.

Rémy took a deep breath and then issued a high-pitched shriek that immediately made the dogs look around. Then she leapt from her perch.

The gravel below gave a harsher landing than the soft sawdust of the circus ring, but Rémy was used to falling hard. She dropped, let herself roll as soon as her feet hit the ground, and was upright again almost immediately. The dogs, having forgotten J, were coming at her fast. She glanced at J, who had frozen in fear.

"Run!" she screamed at him over the sound of the dogs. "Don't stand there — run!"

She didn't wait to see if he did as he was told,

plunging instead along the gravel path that led toward the park's main entrance, the rough stones cutting into her soles. Rémy ignored the pain — it was no worse than the times she'd missed Dominique's back during training. She rounded the south corner of the house and saw the city crowding against the big iron gates. The street lights were beginning to fade into the growing dawn.

Rémy could feel the dogs on her heels as she sprinted the open distance toward her only hope of escape. Behind her, lights had been lit in the big house. All she could do was hope that the staff or their master didn't have a weapon at hand, or there would be something besides the dogs trying to tear holes in her.

By the time she was in reach of the gate, one of the animals was close enough to snap at her heels. Its teeth grazed her leg, leaving a trail of saliva. Rémy used all her remaining strength to jump at the gate, clanging against the wrought iron curlicues and holding on for dear life.

Below her, the dogs had not given up. They howled as their quarry scrambled farther out of reach. They crashed against the metal, their powerful shoulders shaking the gates on their hinges as Rémy struggled to hold on.

She heard shouts behind her, and looked up to see someone leaning out of a high window of the big house. Desperate not to be caught, Rémy dragged herself up the gate, hands and feet gripping the black-painted iron. Twice she almost fell, once dropping far enough to feel the teeth of one of the animals biting into her bare heel before she managed to haul herself away again. But for all her exhaustion, Rémy was still as quick as a fox and twice as agile. Before the men of the house had even gotten out the door she was over the top of the gate and leaping down toward the dirty wet cobbles of the street outside . . . and straight into the arms of the boy with the mismatched eyes.

★ ★ ★

Thaddeus — at the Professor's insistence and out of his generosity, too — had hailed another cab to take him to Lord Abernathy's house. He would have been happy to walk — after all, it was still too early to knock on the door of a peer of the realm, and walking would have served both to clear Thaddeus's head and get him there at a respectable hour. But the Professor had pointed out that strolling around the streets as a wanted man was ill advised and also that it was raining hard. He insisted that arriving dripping wet to converse with a lord would appear odd, and, given Thaddeus's situation, the last thing he needed was to be immediately put at a disadvantage. So the younger man had bowed to the Professor's wisdom and done as he was told.

It meant, however, that he had a lot of time to kill before he could request an audience with Lord Abernathy. He'd bought the early edition of the penny paper but decided to walk a circuit of the outer wall of Abernathy's home before finding a dry patch of wall to lean against as he read it. And so it was that, when the commotion inside started, Thaddeus was on the other side of the wall.

At first he thought a fox had wandered across the dogs' path, sending them into a frenzied bloodlust. But then he heard a weird sound, almost like a scream but at a much higher pitch, and then, in between the baying of the dogs, the sound of feet running on gravel.

He got to the front gate in time to see a small figure dressed in black fling itself at the metal barrier and begin to climb. Assuming that no one leaving a property in such a manner was doing so after lawful entry, Thaddeus stepped forward to apprehend the fleeing criminal.

"Now then," he said as he gripped the surprised

intruder as soon as his feet touched the ground. "What are you up to?"

He found himself, to the astonishment of them both, looking into the shocked and pale face of Rémy Brunel.

"You!"

The girl struggled, trying to pull herself free of his hands. "Let me go!"

Thaddeus snorted with laughter. "Not likely," he told her. "I know what you did. I know what you took! And now you're going to pay for it!"

She fought like a wildcat, in a flurry of limbs and with nails like claws, but Thaddeus wouldn't let go. He was taller, and despite the able muscles he felt in her thin arms, he was stronger, too. He wrestled her against the wall and pinned her there, ignoring the stream of French she spat at him. He suspected the translation may be a little unladylike.

"What are you doing here, eh? Thought you'd come and steal from a defenseless old man, did you? Didn't bank on those dogs though, did you? Now, tell me where the Ocean of Light is." He shook her, running out of patience. "Where have you hidden it?"

"I don't have it," she whispered, still struggling. "You stupid fool! Let me go! I don't have it!"

"Not on you, no — but somewhere. Tell me."

The girl shook her head violently, hair flying around her head. "I did not take it! *Imbécile!* He did!"

Thaddeus frowned. "Who?"

"Abernathy. Your precious Lord. He is the thief, not me!"

Thaddeus laughed again, in disbelief this time. "My God, you circus lot really do know how to spin a yarn, don't you?"

Rémy began to fight him again, but Thaddeus still refused to let her go. He wrapped one arm around her and held her fast against him, using the fingers of his free hand to issue a shrill whistle. A cab drew to a halt on the other side of the street.

"Come on, my girl," he said, the mass of her hair tickling his nose. "It's back to Scotland Yard for you."

"Don't do that, Mr. Rec."

The voice that spoke behind him was thin and reedy. Thaddeus turned to see a young boy standing in the dawn shadows. It was another face Thaddeus recognized.

"J? What the blazes are you doing here?"

The boy pointed at Rémy Brunel, who was currently kicking at Thaddeus's ankles. Thankfully, he was still wearing his police-issue boots.

"I'm wiv 'er, Mr. Rec."

Thaddeus looked between his captive and the street boy. "What? Oh, no, J. I thought we'd talked about this? The last time I caught you? You said, no more burglaries. You said you were going to go to the Sally Ann."

"We weren't stealing! I was just . . . 'elping," J said. "Anyhow, it ain't stealing when the fing is already stole!"

"What?" Thaddeus said, confused.

"I told you, foolish man," growled the defiant girl in his arms. "I did not steal the Darya-ye Noor. Abernathy did."

"I fink you should listen to 'er, Mr. Rec," said J, stepping closer. "That Abernathy, 'e's bad news. And I don't know 'er there too well, but she's a good sort. She bought me breakfast, di'n't she? After I tried to rob 'er, an' all. So, 'ow about you listen? Just for an hour or so, like. You was always good at that, Mr. Rec. Listening."

"I don't have the jewel," said Rémy. "So if you imprison me, you will never get it back."

Thaddeus tried to think, but he couldn't concentrate with the girl still struggling against him. "Stop," he said into her ear. "Please, just stop, for a moment. Let me think."

She calmed then, but he didn't let her go. Thaddeus looked down, saw her bruised and bloodied bare feet, and absently wondered where her shoes were. If he took her back to Glove now, he'd have no more proof in his favor than if he'd hauled a woman chosen at random from the street. And he'd be risking walking back into the lion's den. But the idea that Lord Abernathy could somehow be responsible for all this was preposterous.

Wasn't it?

Chapter 9

AN UNEASY
TRUCE

*T*haddeus stared at J for another moment and then nodded once, sharply. After all, what could he lose by listening? As long as he didn't let the girl out of his sight, he could still take her to the Yard whenever he wanted. And what he really needed was the jewel. If he could make her feel trusted, he might persuade her to give up its hiding place. He'd be in far better a position taking her to Glove with the Darya-ye Noor than without it.

"Very well," he said. "I will listen. But you'll both have to come with me."

The girl swore again, and struggled. "*Non.* It is a trick. I will go nowhere with you. Nowhere!"

"A trick! That's rich, coming from you!"

"Mister Rec," J interrupted. Thaddeus looked at him to see the boy glancing around them uneasily. "It's getting light a bit sharpish, sir. Not sure we should dilly-dally around and about much longer, like."

Rec nodded. "Go and get in the cab, J," he told the boy. "Let's get out of here. I've got somewhere we can go where no one will come looking for us."

★ ★ ★

They arrived back at the Professor's workshop just as the sun was trying to paint the sky a rosy pink instead of its usual all-pervading gray. The air over Limehouse Basin was already thick with noise and smog. The wind had risen with the weak sun, and the sail ropes of the boats moored in the oily water clinked against the masts — *chink-chink-chink* — as if trying to keep the shouts of the dockers to time as they loaded their holds.

"Well, well, well," cried the Professor, as Thaddeus pushed open his door. "I was expecting you to be far longer. Does this bode well? I —" He stopped as Thaddeus led the girl and J inside. "What's this? Visitors?"

"I'm sorry, Professor," Thaddeus told him as he

took the workshop keys from the hook beside the door and locked it. He wasn't risking the girl's escape for anything. "I needed to bring these two somewhere none of us would be found."

The Professor nodded. "Very well," he said, and then looked pointedly at J. The boy's eyes had grown as big as saucers at the sights inside the large room. "On the strict understanding that no one touches anything. Understand, young man?"

Thaddeus watched as J nodded and stuck his hands in his ragged pockets in an uncharacteristic show of obedience. Thaddeus almost smiled. He could remember himself being as awed by the Professor on their first meeting, so many moons ago.

"Good," the Professor beamed. "In that case, welcome, and do have some tea. I've lit the fire, it's so cold a morning. Warm yourselves . . ."

He led the way to the other end of the workshop, to the area that acted as his living room. Thaddeus had rarely seen the Professor anywhere but here in the workshop, and on the nights that he had stayed through the dark hours, working on some elusive invention that he couldn't get quite right, the Professor had always stayed, too. Thaddeus suspected that he didn't have anywhere else to go — this place was his whole life, and where he lived, too. Thaddeus would have gladly swapped his cramped, sooty rooms with Mrs. Carmichael to live here, among the odd and assorted detritus of the Professor's mechanical obsessions.

"My goodness, my dear, what have you done to yourself? Have you no boots?"

The Professor was staring at Rémy's bare feet. Thaddeus realized that one of the dogs must have bitten her — he could see the angry marks of teeth and blood along her left heel — and felt a momentary pulse of guilt when he remembered how roughly he'd dragged her to the cab.

"I lost them," she said quietly, her accent softer now she had stopped shouting. "Inside Abernathy's grounds, when the dogs came."

The Professor frowned. "You broke into Abernathy's home? Who are you?"

"I am nobody," said Rémy, "and I did not break in. But I tried to."

"I've still got yer bag, Rémy," J piped up. "Held on to it as best I could. Fink you've got some slippers in 'ere, ain't yer?"

"Well, you'd best wash your feet before you put them on, at least," Thaddeus told her awkwardly.

She looked up at him, her gaze defiant but still cool, as if to make sure Thaddeus knew that his opinion was not even worth her anger.

"Do you not think I know that?" she asked. "I suppose you think we circus people enjoy the dirt, yes? That even when we are dressed in finery, we long for it?"

He was about to offer to get a bowl of water for her feet when the meaning of her words sank in. "So it was you! At the circus, and at the Tower — Little Bird! I knew it! You did take it, didn't you?" he asked, his anger flaring again. "The Darya-ye Noor. All this nonsense about Lord Abernathy — you were just trying to throw me off the scent. So look, I'm going to give you another chance — and let me tell you, you don't have many of those left, Rémy Brunel. Where is the jewel?"

"I. Do. Not. Have. It," she said very slowly and deliberately.

"Then you sold it. Who to? Where has it gone?"

She shook her head and looked at J. "You said he was a good listener."

"'E usually is," the boy said lamely. "'E's just a bit riled up, ain't 'e? Tell the truth, I don't fink either of you are being much 'elp to the other, are yer?"

"Quite right, my boy, quite right," chipped in the

Professor. "Now, obviously I am a newcomer to these events, but it seems to me that there is a lot of talk with no real meaning. Miss Brunel — it is Miss Brunel, isn't it? Yes. I am going to get you some water and a cloth, and while you bathe your poor feet, you can tell us exactly what happened. Hmm?"

He bustled off as Rémy turned her face to stare into the fire, its orange flames reflected in her large, fierce eyes. The Professor returned a few minutes later with a bowl of water and a towel and placed it in front of the girl, who nodded gratefully and dipped one foot after the other into the welcome warmth.

"Now then," the Professor began. "I've known Thaddeus for a long time. I've watched him grow from a dirty urchin of a boy to become a good and trustworthy man. So, I am going to ask him what it is he has against you because whatever it is, he must have good reason. And then you will have your chance to reply. I gather, Thaddeus, that you think Miss Brunel is at the heart of your misfortunes."

Thaddeus swallowed his anger long enough to reply. "I saw her at the Tower on the night the jewel went missing. I was given it for safe keeping, I saw her face — and then it was gone. She stole it. She's the reason that the police think I am a thief."

The girl looked up at that, and he saw genuine surprise in her eyes. "They blame you?" she asked.

"They think I took it."

She nodded thoughtfully. "Well, then. It seems Lord Abernathy has played us both for fools, Mr. Policeman."

Before Thaddeus could speak again, the Professor held up his hand. "Rémy. Tell us what happened. No lies, do you understand? The truth, my dear. It may not set you free, but it really does make life so much simpler. Yes?"

She stared at the fire again for a moment before nodding. "I was there to take it. The Darya-ye Noor. I tried to take it. I thought I had." She looked up at Thaddeus. "I took it from your pocket. But I did not steal the Darya-ye Noor."

"At last!" Thaddeus exclaimed. "A confession!"

Rémy Brunel shook her head. "You are not listening to me. It was not the Ocean of Light that I took. I thought it was. I had intended to take it. But . . ."

"But?" prompted the Professor.

"When I got back to the circus — when I gave it to my master, to Gustave — he saw that it was a fake. I saw that it was a fake. The stones had been swapped, and that must have happened when the plinth was smashed because the stone I saw under glass was real, I swear it."

"Swapped?" Thaddeus spat, after a moment, "Of course they weren't swapped! What sort of idiot do you take me for?"

Rémy looked up at him. "They were. And if you did not swap them, then it must have been Lord Abernathy. It makes sense, does it not? Who would believe a frail old man, and a lord at that, would stoop so low as to steal? No one, of course. No one did. A perfect crime, you could say, especially since there were others — you and me — to take the blame." There was a brief silence and then she added, "So you see — you and I, Thaddeus Rec — we are the same."

"We are not the same," he said immediately. "We are nothing like the same! I am not a thief. I will never be like you."

She gazed at him steadily, before nodding. "But that is what they are calling you. And you can say whatever you like, but it is what they say that matters in this world. You should know that."

"You set out to take something that was not yours," Thaddeus grated. "Something that you did not earn. Only the worst kind of person — someone who has something wrong with their soul — does that. So now, you will help me get it back — wherever it is — and we will return it to its rightful owner."

Rémy shook her head. "I will get it back," she said, "but I will not return it. I cannot."

Thaddeus threw up his hands in anger. "What is wrong with you? Is this how you like to live your life? On the wrong side of the law, with the lowest people you can find?"

"No," she said, quietly. "But some of us do not have a choice."

"There is always a choice. Always."

Rémy Brunel dried her feet and stood up. Even standing as tall as she could, the top of her head barely reached his shoulder. "Not when you have others depending on you," she said softly. "Not when everything is down to you . . . But you will never understand."

"We are trying to, my dear," said the Professor. "But theft is a hard thing to justify. Why are you so determined to take this jewel?"

"You will never believe me. You will say I am lying, that I am making it up."

"Well, you've got only yourself to blame for that," Thaddeus pointed out.

She made a harsh sound in her throat and turned

away as the Professor sighed and held up his hand. "Tell us anyway, Miss Brunel," he urged. "That can't hurt, can it?"

Rémy stared into the fire a little longer, and then shrugged. "Gustave . . . Gustave said I was cursed. That he was cursed. That he needed the diamond — I do not know, to break the curse, perhaps. He did not get the chance to tell me the whole story." She turned to look Thaddeus in the eye. "You interrupted."

Thaddeus could hardly believe what he was hearing. "My God! A curse now, is it?" He looked at the Professor for help. "She's making it up as she goes along! She'll say anything that she thinks will help her!"

The Professor held up a hand, nodding. "Yes, yes, Thaddeus. And yet . . ."

"And yet? How can there be an 'And yet?'"

His friend ignored him, addressing only the girl. "The Darya-ye Noor is an Indian jewel, am I right?"

"Yes, *monsieur*. It was mined at Golconda."

Thaddeus shook his head. "What difference does it make where the stone came from?"

The Professor crossed his arms. "My dear Thaddeus, while your excellent brain can rarely said to be at fault, what I do sometimes have an issue with is your penchant for conservatism. You would be amazed what can be learned through a willingness to look outside what would be termed the acceptable in polite London circles."

Thaddeus stared at his friend for a moment, and then shook his head. "I don't even know what that means."

The Professor sighed. "All I mean, my dear boy, is that it never hurts to consider the possibilities. I, for example, have been examining new power sources. Steam has transformed our factories, our transport — our lives. But what if there were another, less danger-ous, cleaner, and more productive method of fueling our machines? To this end, I have looked into all sorts of theories and myths — including the elusive stories of the efficacy of gemstones."

For a moment, Thaddeus was stumped. "Precious stones . . . as a power source?"

The Professor shrugged. "To be honest, the idea seems as ludicrous to me as it does to you. But oth-ers believe it, and the myths support it, and belief is, as history has taught us, as immovable as fact in the hearts of those who hold it. And so, if neither of you two stole this gem, we must look at other people who may have taken it. And, my dear Thaddeus, as loath as you are to consider it, it would seem to me that

Lord Abernathy must certainly be at the top of that list."

"Yes!" exclaimed the girl, leaping up. She turned to Thaddeus. "You see! Even he believes me!"

"I didn't say that — yet," warned the Professor. "But what is clear to me is that each of you needs this stone as badly as the other. So, I suggest you find a way to put aside your differences and work together, at least until you've found it. Thaddeus? Do you think you could do that?"

Thaddeus couldn't believe what he was hearing. "This is absurd! We're taking police work into our own hands!"

"And what else do you suggest?" asked Rémy. "That we go to the police, right now, without the jewel? How do you think that would turn out?" She walked toward him, her chin raised high, and stuck out her hand. "Shake hands with me. Shake, and I swear I will help you find the Darya-ye Noor."

"Thaddeus," the Professor urged. "My boy, I believe this is the only way."

Thaddeus shut his eyes briefly. Then he reached out and shook Rémy's hand firmly.

"Good, good!" said the Professor, happily. "Now we're getting somewhere. I'm sure it will take a while for you two to fully trust each other, but I think once you start working together instead of against each other, you'll see that this makes sense."

Thaddeus wasn't so sure and, from her face, neither was his new partner. But the Professor wasn't listening. He'd obviously conjured up a plan.

"Well," said the Professor, "from Miss Brunel's injuries, I think it is safe to say that trying to break into Lord Abernathy's home is inadvisable, to say the least."

"Break in?" Thaddeus said, hardly able to believe what he was hearing. "We're not breaking into any-one's house, let alone a lord's!"

"My dear Thaddeus, your integrity does you credit, I've often said that. But it also leads you to be a little . . . narrow-minded, at times."

"I don't think it's narrow-minded to want to uphold the law!"

"Of course it isn't," his friend soothed, "but when others are not so scrupulous, sometimes the end justi-fies the means. You are looking for one thing, which does not belong to Lord Abernathy any more than it belongs to either of you. If it is not there, you take nothing. Yes? Yes. So, if you cannot break into this man's house, you must find another way of reaching his inner sanctum. That is quite clear. And I think there is one person here who knows just how to do that."

There was a strained silence.

"You mean me, don't yer?" J piped up, fearfully. "You're talkin' about 'is tunnels, ain't yer?"

"Yes, my dear young man, I am. You seem to know quite a good deal about all this. I suspect you may know a way in — a secret entrance, so to speak. Am I right?"

J turned deathly pale and shook his head. "I ain't going near the place. Gives me the creeps, it does."

Thaddeus had no idea what they were talking about and said as much. "Tunnels? What tunnels?"

"The old mines, Mister Rec. Abernathy — 'e's up to somethin' down there."

"Mines? There aren't any mines under London. Certainly not around here, at any rate."

The Professor crossed his arms and raised his eyebrows. "No? Are you sure about that?"

"Well — of course I am! How could there be?"

"Oh, you'd be surprised what you'll find under this city, my boy. It's been here a very, very long time. And more has disappeared into its foundations than people even knew existed." The Professor turned back to J.

"Well, my boy? Could you take these two down there? Safely, I mean?"

As Thaddeus watched, J swallowed hard. "I — I don't fink so, Mister Professor. I bin there once, and that was enough for me. It ain't safe. I said I ain't never going back, and I don't want to, sir. I don't want to."

Thaddeus rested a hand on his shoulder. "Now, now, J — there's no need to get upset. What old wives' tale has got you so scared?"

"It ain't no ol' wives' tale, Mr. Rec," J gulped. "I seen it wiv me own eyes, I 'ave. And me mate, Tommy — 'e went missin', like the others. 'E's down there somewhere. I know 'e is. I should go to get 'im out, but I'm too scared o' gettin' caught meself . . ."

Thaddeus knelt in front of the terrified child. He had no idea what all this talk was, but he hated to see this boy — who had already seen enough in his short life — so unhappy.

"J," he said. "Listen to me. You can trust me. You know that, don't you? Haven't I always done right by you?" J nodded and sniffed. "Right. So, whatever's going on, you can tell me. What's all this about your friend?"

J shook his head, a resigned look on his face. "It ain't no good, Mr. Rec. Telling you, I mean. You ain't never going to understand unless you sees it for your-self." He looked at the Professor. "I knows that, Mister Professor. I does."

The Professor slapped him gently on the back. "Good boy, J. You're a brave lad. Do you know what? How about, when you get back, I show you all of my inventions? You know, let you see how they all work?"

The boy's mouth dropped open, his fear instantly forgotten. "What — really?"

"Most definitely, J," said the Professor. "I think you're a clever boy. Maybe you'll even give me a hand with a few puzzles I have yet to solve, eh?"

J straightened his shoulders and wiped his nose on the back of his cuff. "Right then. Well — what are we waitin' for, eh? Let's go!"

The Professor chuckled. "Hold your horses, my lad. First, I think you all need a bit of a rest. Besides, the tide is in, and for where you need to go, I think it needs to be out. Am I right?"

J's shoulders sagged a little. "Oh," he said, "yeah, you're right. It does."

"Well then, while we're waiting — Miss Brunel . . ."

"Yes, *monsieur*?"

"My dear, you may want to look through the large wooden chest in the office over there," the Professor pointed to his private room, closed off at the back of the workshop. "Over the years I have collected various garments that may be of . . . of use to you. I think there are some boots, too. Do please take anything else that you like, while you're at it. It's only going to waste where it is. Oh, and pick a new outfit for our young lad J, too, would you? In the meantime, I have a few items to gather together for your trip."

★ ★ ★

Rémy could hardly wait to investigate the chest. She tried not to look at Thaddeus Rec. Part of her felt guilty for the fact that he was in trouble because of a theft that she would have performed herself if not for Lord Abernathy's treachery. But by far the larger part of her was just enraged by him. By the fact that he had caught her, by the fact that he would not listen . . . even by his face! It annoyed her, those mismatched eyes that refused to believe a word she said, whether she was telling the truth or not, even though she had agreed to help him. And it annoyed her more that she didn't know why it made her so angry.

She should try to escape, she knew that. Rémy had agreed to work with Thaddeus Rec only because she couldn't see another way out of her predicament, but she'd be better off alone. She always was. Still, Rémy was not one to look a gift horse in the mouth. It had been a long, long time since she'd had new clothes, and the idea that there was a chest of garments from which she could take her pick was too good an opportunity to pass up, especially now she had lost her trusty boots.

Rémy opened the door to the Professor's office cautiously, looking over her shoulder at Thaddeus, who glowered at her from his place beside the fire. She turned her back on him and slipped inside. It was no tidier here than in the main workshop. Nuts and bolts, springs and wires, clock faces and barometers — there were piles of them all over the place, on the floor and beside the books stacked one against the other on the bookcase, and on the large wooden desk that dominated the space. There was a mirror, too, and a washbasin, still full of water.

She paused, fascinated by the sight of an array of pots of color, like the greasepaints she used to turn herself into Little Bird. These were not so bright, though. They were flesh-tones, in various tints, and they were set beside strange, soft, molded noses and ears and feathery false eyebrows. It reminded her of the circus, and of Colicos the clown, who could change his appearance as often as the wind changed the weather. *Who exactly is this Professor friend of Rec's?* Rémy asked herself. He acted like a gentleman, but lived like a peddler. She wasn't sure she trusted him. But then, life had taught her not to trust anyone. Maybe she should begin to learn.

Rémy searched for the trunk and found it under a pile of old, yellowing maps. It was stout, made of wood the color of walnuts, and banded with strips of iron. It was not locked, though, and the lid swung open easily enough. Inside were piles of clothes of all descriptions and for all ages and sizes, both male and female. For a second, Rémy was stunned. And then she began to rummage.

The clothes were mostly black shirts and trousers, but here and there among them were flashes of color. Rémy pulled out a corset of black satin and stared at it. It reminded her of the costumes she wore on the trapeze, and she loved it instantly. She also picked up a short-sleeved black top that would go under it perfectly. There were several pairs of boys' trousers, too — they would be far more practical than a skirt. She found the smallest pair she could — they were worn, but still had plenty of life in them — and dragged them out. Finally she found a short black jacket whose only fault was a small tear in the bottom hem. No one would notice though, so it would do nicely. Dressing quickly, she was relieved to find that most things fitted her well. She had to cinch in the waist of the trousers with a rough leather belt, but the top and jacket were perfect, and the corset added a touch of bravado that made her feel as if she were about to perform. And if ever there was a time when Rémy felt brave, it was when she was about to step out onto the wire.

Pulling on a pair of boots that were only slightly too big, Rémy went back out into the workshop, holding a new pair of trousers and a shirt for J. It was quiet save for the crackle of the fire. She looked toward the door and wondered if the policeman had remembered to lock it this time. She couldn't see the Professor anywhere. Maybe this was her chance, if she could . . .

She stopped as her eyes fell on Thaddeus. He was sitting in one of the old armchairs, gazing at J, who had fallen asleep in the chair closest to the blazing fire. As she watched, Thaddeus got up to pick up her cloak and place it carefully over the boy. He glanced up as he returned to his chair and saw her. They stared at each other for a moment before Thaddeus looked toward the door.

"It's locked," he told her quietly. "I'm not quite as stupid as you think I am."

"I never thought you were stupid."

He smiled wryly and touched his cheek where her nails had caught him a glancing blow during their struggle. "Funny. That's not what you said earlier."

Rémy gave up on the idea of escape and headed for the fire. "Where is your friend, the Professor?" she asked.

"Gone to get us some food."

She nodded. "He is a kind man."

"Yes, he is."

She could feel Thaddeus's eyes on her as she sat in front of the fire. He seemed to have only just noticed her change of clothes.

"What?" she asked. "Not smart enough for you?"

He looked away. "Just surprised you'd choose to wear that thing. I thought most women hated them."

She grinned, glancing down at her corset. "Well," she said, "I am not 'most' women. Besides, I think it suits me."

Thaddeus dropped back into his chair. "I never said it didn't," he muttered, almost too low for her to hear.

Chapter 10

THE DEPTH OF
THE EARTH

They left some hours later, as twilight coincided with the turning of the tide. After they had eaten, Thaddeus had managed to doze a little, and he felt better for it. When he'd woken, the first person he'd looked for had been Rémy Brunel, in case she had fled in his sleep. He didn't have to look far — she was curled up on the hearth, like a cat, her arms wrapped around her knees and her hair strewn out about her head. As he watched her, she woke and sat up, blinking at him. He pretended he'd been staring at the fire.

The Professor appeared again, this time with three small packs which he passed to each of them.

"Just some essentials," said Thaddeus's friend.

"Candles, matches, a draught of water each — that kind of thing."

"Thanks, Professor," Thaddeus said as he took his. "And what about that listening device you planted in my pocket? Could we use that, too?"

"I wish you could, my boy," said the Professor, "but where you are going, even if you managed to also carry the attending set with you, I doubt the signal would pass. What I can give you, though, are these."

He pointed to a nearby work bench. On it lay three sets of the night-vision glasses.

Thaddeus went to them. "Professor!" he exclaimed. "You got them to work?"

"Indeed, and I think you should each have a pair to take with you. Where you're going, they will no doubt come in very useful. Though there will still be levels of darkness that not even they can banish, which is why I have given you each a candle. A single flame should be enough to help the glasses work, even if they seem to have failed completely."

Thaddeus, Rémy, and J set off as dusk fell, J leading them around the edge of the Basin and turning left along Narrow Street, past The Grapes. Thaddeus couldn't imagine where they were going. He'd never heard of mines under the East End of London.

J took them east, following the Thames as it meandered on its long journey to the sea. It wasn't until they reached Lime Kiln Wharf that J slowed and looked about him. Then he slipped down a tiny, greasy alley that disappeared toward the river. It was so narrow that the dying light of day barely filtered down to the rough cobble and dirt path beneath their feet.

The walkway ended at the Thames. The river's shore lay below them at the end of a metal ladder that stopped just above the exposed mud and sand. The tide was out and the water had receded to its lowest point, leaving a wide beach at either side. If the tide had been in, the bottom of the ladder would have led straight into the murky water.

"We can't go down there," Thaddeus said. "The mudlarks own the river bank. They won't like it."

"Mudlarks?" Rémy queried.

"The beachcombers of London," Thaddeus told her. "They own whatever they find on the shore. It's been that way for centuries."

The French girl sniffed. "That cannot be a very good living. And to have to work with this smell always in your nose!"

"Oh, you'd be surprised at the valuables what washes up 'ere, Miss," said J. "But don't you worry

yerself, Mister Rec. The 'larkers, they know me. Stick
with me and they'll treat you right."

Thaddeus nodded reluctantly and watched as the
boy made his way down the ladder, the new shirt
that Rémy had given him flapping in the wind that
rose from the water. He sent Rémy down next, still
suspecting she may run the moment he was preoccupied. She skipped down the metal rungs as if it were a
gentle slope, not a slippery plunge to a nasty death. He
wished he had her confidence with heights. Thaddeus
had always preferred to have his feet squarely on solid
ground.

He followed gingerly, his knuckles white as they
gripped the cold metal tightly after each step. At the
bottom, his feet sank in the wet sand. They set off
together, keeping close to the walls built along the riverbank, on which stood the busy wharves and docks.
The walls were carpeted in the velvet green of moss
kept damp by the constant drenching of the river at
high tide.

J nodded to a man who stood by the water's edge.
He was dressed in several layers of clothing that
were uniformly brown, and his boots looked as black
and greasy as the sediment beneath them. He could
almost have been a feature of the river shore himself, a

barnacled spit of sand, merely man-shaped. The mud-lark raised his hand slowly at them in greeting, and then turned back to the net at his feet. It was on a long pole, and he dragged it slowly over the damp sand, searching for anything that may be of value, if not to him, then to someone else.

The shore was uneven, dotted with fallen bricks and rough stones and pocked with the castings-off from a thousand ships. Thaddeus kept his eyes on his footing. There were shells, shards of pottery, and pieces of cutlery. He saw clay pipes everywhere, the sort that were smoked a handful of times and then thrown away. He wondered where they had all started off. Had they washed down the river or been thrown from one of the warehouses above?

Through his brief reverie he heard a shout carried over the wind and looked up to see that J was far ahead, with Rémy a distance away between them. The boy was waving his arm, urging them on. Thaddeus picked up his pace.

The boy was waiting for them beside the wide mouth of a small tunnel, no bigger than a large pipe, that led directly into the brick wall below the basement of a cotton wharf. It was built a short distance above the sand bank, and so when the tide was in, it must have been fully submerged. A trickle of brown water was dripping from it and onto the sand.

"In there?" Thaddeus asked.

"Yup," said J. "Sorry, Mister Rec, but it's the only way. We better be quick, too — once the tide turns, it'll fill with water, and we've got a long way to go."

The boy pulled out his glasses and put them on. Rémy did the same. "Come on, then," she said. "What are we waiting for? Let's get on with it!"

The boy ducked his head and jumped inside, his feet splashing in the brackish water. Rémy went in next, not even pausing to glance at Thaddeus. Watching her receding figure, he almost had the feeling she was beginning to enjoy herself.

Thaddeus slipped on his night glasses and took a deep breath before he followed. Once in the pipe, the outside world vanished at once. The tunnel reeked of wetness. The brick walls were slick with slime and very cold. His shoes were damp within seconds as he pushed on through the sludge. Ahead of him, Rémy seemed to have no such worries — the new boots the Professor had given her must have been more water-tight than his own.

J forged ahead at surprising speed. The sewer was not straight, and at first it rose so steeply that

Thaddeus found himself having to pull himself up. It leveled out soon enough but twisted and turned so rapidly that Thaddeus soon lost his sense of direction. Then it began to tilt downward again, lower and lower into the earth, but he had no idea how far. His glasses cast everything in a strange green glow that was strong enough only to stop him stumbling on the uneven brick. Every now and then, either J or Rémy would turn and look back at him, their eyes two weird, glowing discs of greenish light in the murk.

Thaddeus wondered how long it would take for the river to follow them up the tunnel once the tide turned. He knew how fast the water could cover the shore — it was one reason he never liked going down onto the sand. He'd almost been caught when he was a boy. He hadn't seen the water coming until he'd turned around and realized his way back was cut off, and with no other way out. He'd clung to one of the wooden bulwarks for hours, his arms aching until at every second he thought they would give out. It was only luck that saved him — a passing eel fisherman spotted his plight and pulled him to the safety of his tiny boat.

Thaddeus was so lost in that memory that he didn't realize Rémy had stopped. He collided with her, knocking her off balance. She yelped and he reached out, anxious to steady her before she fell. He caught her around the waist until she regained her footing.

"Sorry," he said, struck — and not for the first time — by how very small she was.

"Clumsy oaf," she muttered. As she put her hands over his to push him away, he was surprised by their warmth. He had come to think of her as a cold creature, somehow. "Watch where you are going, yes?" she said, her voice softening a little.

"Why have we stopped?" He peered over her shoulder. The tunnel had come to an end, opening into deeper darkness that even their night glasses could not penetrate.

He felt Rémy pat his shoulder, as if to comfort his nerves. He turned to look at her, taken aback by the gentle reassurance. She had obviously surprised herself, too, because she looked away immediately, dropping her hand.

"Don't go no further," J warned, standing at the very mouth of the darkness. "There's a fall down there'd break yer neck."

"What do we do now?" Rémy asked, frustrated. "These glasses are broken!"

"No," said Thaddeus, "they just require a little more light. Isn't that what the Professor said? That's why he gave us the candles."

"Tha's right, Mr. Rec," said J, brightening. "That Professor, 'e finks of everyfing."

Thaddeus took his pack from around his shoulders and pulled a short, fat white candle from its depths, along with a slim box of matches. "I'll light mine — you two save yours," he said. "They won't last long."

Thaddeus struck a match and held it to the candle's wick. The yellow glow of the flame gleamed white and pale green in front of his night glasses. He stepped back, leaving the candle standing on the rough stone floor.

Rémy gasped. Thaddeus turned to see what she was looking at, the glow of the candle giving the glasses just enough light to illuminate the dark space before them.

The darkness had hidden a space that opened before them like a vast wasteland. The level where they stood dropped to a floor more than a hundred and fifty feet below, cut out of the clay of London itself. Above them was more rock, as if they had stumbled into a cave. Except they obviously were not the first to find this place, not by a very long shot.

The giant room was crowded, but not with people. It was almost like a larger version of the Professor's workshop, but more orderly, and the more terrifying for it. The space was filled with large structures of the like Thaddeus had never seen before but somehow recognized. In one corner were rows of what seemed to be modern suits of armor. They were made of shining silver metal, with mechanical parts at their knees and arms and glass domes to completely enclose the wearer's head. Each had a tube leading to a patterned metal cylinder, strapped to the back. There were at least a hundred of them.

Beside the suits stood something that looked almost like a boat, though the deck was completely encased in a double layer of glass so that anyone operating it would have seemed to be inside a bubble. In the glass had been cut portholes made of silver — not to see out of but to let in air, Thaddeus supposed — and they matched its body, riveted together from sheets of clean, taintless metal.

There were steam engines — two of them, though they were like no locomotives that Thaddeus had ever seen. There were no tracks leading to them. Instead, they had great wheels like those on the most basic cart, but made of metal rather than wood. The wheels were bound together by huge strips of leather, studded with bolt heads filed into savage, shiny points.

There were so many machines like these that Thaddeus could not take them all in. To him, they were terrifying, but magnificent.

"*Mon Dieu!*" Rémy whispered beside him. "What are they?"

Thaddeus shook his head, as awed as Rémy was. He realized that the tunnel they had been in, rather than opening onto a sheer drop as he'd first thought, actually led onto a small wooden platform, about ten feet deep. It was enclosed almost completely by a metal handrail, apart from a gap directly before them that was about the same width as the tunnel. Immediately to their left there were steep narrow steps cut out of the stone, leading down to the lower floor. In the rough wall above the top step had been set some kind of large lever. It looked like the sort used on the docks at Limehouse, to turn the winches on and off. Thaddeus stepped forward onto the wooden platform to get a better look at the wondrous cave, Rémy and J following his lead.

Directly below them was another huge machine. It looked almost like a diving bell, but was a hundred times the size.

Thaddeus leaned over the thin rail at the platform's edge, trying to get a closer look.

"Amazin' eh?" J said quietly. "Scary, but amazin' all the same."

"What are they?" Thaddeus asked. "What is this place?"

"Somewhere we were never meant to see," Rémy said in a hushed voice. Thaddeus looked at her and was surprised to see fear in her eyes.

"And all this — this is Abernathy's doing?" Thaddeus asked.

"Oh, yeah. You ain't seen nothin' yet, neither," said J, turning to move from the platform toward the steps. "Come on, let's —"

There was a scuffing sound as J tripped over the candle. He swore as it skittered away, the candlelight flickering violently as it rolled, bouncing down the steps. J lunged after it, trying to stop it before the light was snuffed out completely. Thaddeus saw him lose his balance and reach out to steady himself against the wall.

"J!" Thaddeus and Rémy shouted as one, as they saw the boy's searching hands grasp hold of the metal lever. But their warning came too late. Just as the candle went out, there was the sound of old, disused metal scraping as it moved.

"Oh, bleeding 'eck!" cried J through the darkness.

There was a sudden groaning noise, the sound of metal shearing against metal, and a whir so loud it shook the platform on which they stood.

"What's that?" Thaddeus shouted over the noise. Then he looked down between the wooden planks that made up the platform. "Oh, my God — that machine — that machine has started up!"

It was true. The mighty contraption below them was creaking into life like a huge, metal giant. An eerie blue light, brighter than phosphorus, glowed below them. There was an upward blast of heat, too, as if someone had lit a fire. No, not just a fire, it was too intense for that. It was a furnace.

And then the platform began to tip. Thaddeus felt it, falling away from beneath his feet. He stumbled and reached out to catch the rail as he heard Rémy scream.

"J," she cried, "the lever! Push it back up! Push it back up!"

"I'm trying," J cried. "It's stuck! It won't move! Quick, back into the tunnel! We got to —" But it was already too late. The platform must have been on some sort of mechanical hinge, because it jerked and then began to tip, and even if they had been able to scramble to the top of the platform, the gap would have been too great to cross. A moment later, Thaddeus felt himself begin to slide down the smooth wooden planks of the platform, down toward the cold rock floor of the vast room. Below him, he could see the machine opening like the jaws of a great, metal beast, ready to devour them all.

"Thaddeus!"

At her cry, Thaddeus looked up at Rémy. Nimble as ever, she had wrapped her arms and legs around the narrow section of handrail at the top of the platform. She was reaching one hand out toward him.

"Catch my hand," she shouted over the noise of metal and wood. "I can pull you up! Quickly!"

"I'm too heavy!"

"I am stronger than I look! Be quick!"

He tried to reach for her, but he was too far away. Their fingers brushed but could not grasp. He saw her let go with her arms completely, until only her legs were around the rail, as if she were back in the circus tent. Her hands caught his wrists, but he knew at once that she should let him go.

"I can't," he said. "Rémy, it's too dangerous. You'll fall . . ."

"I can hold you!"

"Don't worry about me! Get J!"

The terrified boy was clinging to the opposite rail, trying to scramble over the side to the steps that led down to the floor. The platform was almost vertical now. It reached its apex with a sudden, sharp, jarring jerk that shook them all.

Rémy screamed again as Thaddeus slipped from her grasp.

Chapter 11

TRAPPED

$\mathcal{R}$émy watched helplessly as Thaddeus plummeted off the end of the platform and into the depths of the machine below. There was a whirring sound and it began to shut, two halves sliding together until they were a seamless whole. The policeman disappeared from sight, trapped inside a riveted silver monster.

"Rémy!" She looked up to see J still clinging to the rail, a horrified look on his face.

The platform began to right itself again. Rémy held on to the rail until it was back in place, stunned by what had just taken place. It had all happened so quickly. One minute Thaddeus was there, the next he'd gone, just like that.

"'E's going to roast! Look at them flames!" J sobbed as Rémy ran down the stairs toward the contraption.

The machine was cylindrical but tapered to a point at the end that had opened to swallow Thaddeus. It had a large window in its side, but she couldn't see through it. The machine was standing on struts, also made of metal. Between the struts, fire belched in three great streams so hot that the center of the flames burned white as they hit the scorched ground.

"It's my fault," J wailed, stumbling after her. "It's my fault!"

She turned to him. "It was an accident, J. Just an accident."

"I started it off! I didn't mean to!"

The poor boy was crying piteously now, staring at the machine with tears cutting through the dirt on his face. Rémy crouched down in front of him, gripping his shoulders.

"J, listen to me. He is not dead."

"But look at them flames!"

"There's a window, J. Why would there be a window if it was not supposed to have people inside? Hmm?"

J blinked, looking at the metal monstrosity as his tears stopped. "Cor," he said. "You're right."

"He is trapped, yes? We must get him out. And turn it off. "

"But the lever's broke," whimpered J. "It won't budge, Rémy, not for nothing."

"There must be another way," said Rémy, hoping against hope she was right. "A machine that big, they would not have only one lever, yes? Think, J, think! The last time you were here. Can you think of anything you might have seen? More levers, somewhere else?"

J swiped a hand at his damp face. He looked blank for a moment and then brightened up, nodding. "Yeah! Yeah, there are more levers, right enough. This way!"

Rémy followed him across the room, toward the far wall. She'd lost her night glasses, dropping them from the platform as she'd tried to save Thaddeus from falling, but luckily, seeing her way wasn't a problem. The belching flames of the machine sent out a hot, bright glow that illuminated the cavern and cast huge, menacing shadow-shapes against the walls.

Although Rémy had tried to sound confident when she reassured J, she felt anything but — her heart was pounding and she felt sick. Thaddeus couldn't be dead. He couldn't — could he? Not just like that, not so fast, not so suddenly. Rémy kept seeing his face as he fell away from her. He must have been scared, but he hadn't made a sound. The last words he'd spoken had been to tell her to save J rather than himself. A brave man, indeed.

"'Ere," J said, sniffling, as they arrived at a bank of four huge metal levers. "But how do we know what one is the right one? Or if any of 'em are? They might all be for somethin' else."

"We will just have to try them all," said Rémy, though her heart was pounding. What if they started up another of these awful monstrosities? What if they made things even worse for Thaddeus? But what other choice did she have? Rémy and J grasped one each, and pushed them down. Nothing happened.

"It must be one of these," Rémy said, of the last two. She pushed one and a huge light swelled into the cave, so bright it almost drowned out the bonfire brightness of the flames.

"Not that one!" J said, panicked.

"*D'accord, d'accord* . . ." Rémy pulled it back down, and the incredible light died again. She grabbed the final lever and wrestled with it, forcing it into position. This had to be it, or . . .

At first, nothing happened. The flames continued to belch, giving off a tremendous heat that could be felt even across the room. But then they began to sputter. One by one they guttered out.

"Yes!" J cried, jubilant.

Rémy wasn't ready to celebrate yet. She went back to the machine, looking for a way in. There was one panel that wasn't riveted — could it be a door? She pushed at it, but it did not budge and there was no handle. Rémy thumped against it, and then placed her ear to the smooth silver panel. She could hear nothing — the cylinder might as well have been solid inside. The metal was mysteriously cool, as if the flames below had had no effect on it at all.

"J," she said. "Search for something that we can use to pry this open. Anything. Quickly!"

J ran off as she went to the window. It seemed to be covered in something that made it milky and unclear. She frowned, frustrated and bemused — why have a window that was impossible to see through? She thumped against the glass, trying to peer through. If there was a door, why hadn't he used it yet? Unless . . . unless he really was dead . . . She pushed the lingering thought away.

"Thaddeus!" Rémy shouted. "Thaddeus Rec! Can you hear me? Can you see me? Are you — are you alive?"

There was no answer except from J, who appeared at her side, puffing hard and with empty hands. "There's nothin'," he said. "Nothin' I can lift, anyways. And what do you mean, is 'e alive? You said —"

Rémy held up her hand. "Let me think, J. Just — let me think."

J obediently fell silent as Rémy looked around the room again. She noticed three tunnels leading out of the cavern and into darkness. How far would they have to walk down each of them before they found something that could help them get into the machine? Then her gaze fell upon the empty suits that stood in silent rows. They had been fashioned out of the same silvery metal that made up the machine's panels, making them impenetrable. At the joints were cogs and gears, presumably to make their weight easier to move. Though the suits seemed to be mechanical, they didn't look as if they could move on their own. They were hollow inside, so surely they must have been designed for a person to wear.

What if she put one on? If she did, her hands would be encased in metal and would become big and heavy. Would she then be strong enough to punch a hole through this infernal contraption? Could her fingers possibly pry open that door? Or perhaps even the metal trap that Thaddeus had fallen though, if she could climb up to it in the suit? But would she even be able to work out how to control it, once inside?

* * *

Thaddeus watched from inside the machine. He banged on the glass and shouted, but they didn't seem to hear him. He couldn't understand why. Rémy had walked right up to the glass and looked in, but her eyes stared through him as if blind. How could she not see? She'd been staring right at him!

He'd watched as they'd worked out how to turn off the flames. The heat from them must have been intense, but he couldn't feel it. It was as if the skin of the machine deflected the heat, so that the interior was completely cool and comfortable.

Well, not exactly comfortable. Thaddeus had hit his head as he'd fallen, and the gash above his eye was still bleeding. He looked around for something to hold over the cut, but there was nothing. He pulled his sleeve over his hand and held that to his head, instead.

"Rémy," he shouted again, as she stood at the window, staring up at the machine. It looked as if she were contemplating scaling it. "Rémy! I'm here! I'm here!"

He looked around him. Everything was strange

and out of place. There was a chair, but it was fixed to the wall of the machine, directly below the window rather than facing it, so that it pointed up toward the angled ceiling, the one through which Thaddeus had fallen. That had sealed shut so solidly that it looked as if it would never open again. In front of the chair was a curved silver desk, covered in tiny levers, dials, and switches. There were silver cabinets fixed to the walls. As he looked at them now, it seemed as if he was seeing them sideways. It was almost as if the entire machine was designed to tilt, so that what was now the wall would become the floor.

Thaddeus began to feel claustrophobic — as if he'd been buried alive. Every time he shouted, his voice fell like a lead weight, dead against the metal. He noticed what looked like a door in one of the walls. It had a handle, but it wouldn't budge, even though he pulled with all his might. He struggled up to the chair and into it, pulling lever after lever, but there was no response. It were as if the machine was completely dead. Perhaps turning off the flames below had cut off all power to its insides, too.

He scrambled back down to the floor, looking out of the window to see that Rémy and J had moved. They were no longer standing in front of the machine.

Thaddeus's heart turned over as he saw Rémy examining one of the strange armored suits on the other side of the room. What was she doing? She wasn't seriously considering getting into one of them, surely?

"Rémy!" he shouted, banging on the glass again. "Don't do it! It's not safe! You don't know —"

He broke off as he watched J, who had suddenly become animated. The boy had grabbed Rémy's arm and was trying to pull her away, pointing in the direction of one of the three tunnels that led out of the room. Had he heard someone coming? If he had . . .

"Run!" Thaddeus shouted through the glass, banging his hand flat against it. "Rémy! J! You mustn't be caught. Get out — run!"

J was obviously telling Rémy the same thing, but she held back. She looked toward the machine again and then pulled her arm out of J's grip, running back toward Thaddeus. She ran right up to the glass, banging, shouting for him. He couldn't hear her, and she obviously still couldn't see him.

"Just go," he cried, even though he knew she couldn't hear. "I'll be all right. Look after yourself. Look after J. Just go!"

Rémy fell still and stared through the glass. For a moment, Thaddeus thought she could see him. She flattened her hands against the window, and he realized that if the glass hadn't been between them, they would have been no more than two inches apart. He reached out, hesitantly, pressing one hand and then the other to the cold ghosts of hers.

She said something, her lips moving silently. And although he couldn't hear her, he knew what she'd said, as surely as if she'd spoken straight into his ear.

"I'll come back," she said. "I'll come back for you, Thaddeus Rec. I promise."

He felt a strange sensation in his chest. There was a jolt, as if something had been plunged deeply into his heart and had lodged there. Thaddeus blinked.

"Go," he whispered. "Please, Rémy — go."

She stepped back almost as if she'd heard, staring at the glass for a moment longer. Then she turned and ran. J didn't wait for her, careering ahead and disappearing down one of the tunnels with Rémy close behind. They vanished into the darkness.

Seconds later, a group of men appeared from the tunnel on the far right. There were four of them, tall and broad-shouldered. They were dressed in loose black trousers and shirts, their faces covered up to the eyes, and their heads wrapped in black turbans. Across their chests were strapped wide leather belts, a hunter's pouch on each. They moved in formation, two ahead and two behind. One of the men in front held up his hand and they all stopped in unison. This leader gave brief signs with his hands and they separated. They were searching.

Thaddeus stepped away from the window, moving backward until his shoulders touched the cabinet behind him. Three of the men had walked out of sight. But the leader seemed to know exactly where to go. He glanced up at something above the machine — the wooden platform, Thaddeus supposed. Then he walked straight toward the window.

For a moment, the man stared in blindly, as Rémy had done just a few moments before. Then he pulled out a pair of tinted glasses from his hunter's pouch. He put them on and peered solemnly at the glass.

The leader shouted something briefly. In seconds, the three other men stood beside him, all wearing glasses and all looking in. And this time, he knew they could see him.

Thaddeus was caught.

Chapter 12

DARK DISCOVERIES

$\mathcal{R}$émy followed J into the dark tunnel. She could now hardly see where she was going. She had to put her hands out against the narrow walls to stop herself stumbling on the rough ground. Ahead of her, J, still wearing his glasses, was more sure of himself. He ran on, turning corner after corner before eventually stopping. She drew to a halt beside him, putting out a hand in the dark to find his small shoulder as he bent and caught his breath.

"We should have gone back into the sewer," she said after a moment. "Back to the river shore."

"We'd never 'ave made it out before the tide turned," said J. "'Old on a mo' . . ."

Rémy heard rummaging and then the sound of a match being struck. The flame flickered in the darkness, illuminating J's thin face as he touched it to the thick candle he'd pulled from his pack. She sighed in relief, and the light blossomed, yellow in the narrow passageway.

J pulled his glasses down around his neck and tried to smile, though his eyes were dark with worry. "Mr. Rec . . ."

Rémy's stomach turned over. "I know. But we'll get him back, J. I promise. Maybe they will not discover him where he is, in the belly of the machine."

J nodded but didn't look convinced. "Well, I reckon we're going to 'ave to get out some'ow," he said. "Go back to the Professor, see what he can do to 'elp."

"Do you know another way out of here?"

"No," J admitted. "But there's got to be another way, ain't there? Stands to reason. And —"

He stopped suddenly, the flame from the candle light casting lined shadows on his face as he frowned. J turned his head, listening.

"J?" Rémy asked. "What is it?"

"Do you 'ear that?"

They fell silent for a moment. At first Rémy could hear nothing. She was about to tell J as much when it came to her. A faint, echoing sound like wood being struck with an axe, but tinnier.

Rémy straightened up. The sound was echoing down the tunnel they were in. It seemed a long way away. "Come on," she said.

"You ain't plannin' on going toward it?"

She looked at the boy and shrugged. "Do you have a better idea? That could be coming from the surface, for all we know."

As they set off along the corridor, Rémy tried not to think about Thaddeus and what had happened to him. She didn't know why it bothered her so much. After all, with him trapped, she was free. It just didn't seem the victory that it should have been, somehow.

Ahead of her, J turned the corner and then stopped suddenly, blowing out the candle and plunging them back into darkness.

"J!" Rémy exclaimed, "What —"

"Shh!" he hissed.

She fell silent, blinking in the blackness. Then as her eyes adjusted, she realized it wasn't as dark as it had been. There was a faint glow — and the sound they had heard was louder now.

"Come on," she whispered, taking the lead.

They crept along the shaft. It was becoming

narrower, so narrow, in fact, and so low that Rémy had to stoop to keep going. The glow became brighter and the noise more pronounced, until they could eventually see where it was coming from — an opening in the tunnel to their left.

Rémy glanced back at J to see fear etched on his face. She knew what he was thinking. They obviously hadn't found a way to the surface, and the sounds were most definitely those of industry — heavy, resounding clangs, dull thuds, and the shouts of men's voices.

"Let's turn back," he said. "Eh? Let's find another route, Rémy. Back there, I fink I saw . . ."

Rémy shook her head. "I must see what they're doing!"

She moved to the edge of the light, not stepping fully into it. She peered around the doorway.

"Mon Dieu!"

The doorway she stood in was halfway up the wall of what seemed to be an underground quarry. Rough-hewn steps led down onto the mine floor, which was deep and black with streaks of metal that she could have mistaken for silver if she hadn't known they were under the city of London. There were people everywhere, hacking at the quarry face, dragging chunks of rock hewn out of the earth to rough wooden carts set on tracks that led up and out of a larger tunnel on the opposite wall.

"Let me see," she heard J say behind her. She moved to make space for him and he looked, struck speechless by the sight before him.

The people working the rock face were dirty and painfully thin. They were both men and women, dressed in rags and with chains binding their bare feet together. Children no older than J toiled in the dust, too. Guards stood around the edges of the cavern holding huge, flaming torches that matched the ones pinned to the wall. One stood casually eating an apple while a hungry child looked on. When he caught her staring, he lunged toward her and she screamed, scurrying back to her work.

"The man who owns this must be the devil himself," Rémy whispered.

J wasn't listening. He was silently watching one of the workers down below. Then suddenly he jerked forward, making as if to run into the light and down the steps. Rémy managed to catch him, dragging him back before he gave them both away.

"What are you doing?" she whispered, as the boy struggled in her arms. "J, are you mad? Stop it!"

"I seen 'im!" J whispered back, fighting against her. "I seen 'im, down there! I got to get 'im out!"

"Who?" Rémy asked, thinking for one confused moment that he meant Thaddeus. "Who have you seen?"

"Tommy!" the boy cried. "Me best mate, Tommy. Let me go!"

"J, I can't. If you go down there, you'll be caught. We'll probably both be caught! We cannot help anyone if they catch us. Stop it. Stop struggling, J. Listen to me!"

J fell still abruptly, nodding. Rémy loosened her grip cautiously and moved to block his path, just in case the boy tried to run again.

"I can't leave 'im there," J said tearfully. "'E's my best mate! I can't just . . . leave 'im."

"I understand," Rémy soothed. "I know it is hard. But we won't leave them. Not any of them — not your friend, not those other people, not Thaddeus. We will get them out. But we can't do it alone. We have to get out of here, J. Yes? Be patient, please."

He stared at her for another moment before nodding. "Alright. But let's be quick about it. I ain't leavin' 'im down there for a minute longer than I can 'elp. Got it?"

Rémy nodded. They slipped through the light, keeping as low as possible, and then continued along the stone tunnel. Rémy was nervous now — these passageways were obviously used and if someone came the other way, they would have nowhere to go. She came to a crossroads in the rock passage and turned left. They had only gone a few more paces before J stopped. She turned to look at him.

"What is it?"

His eyes were large and fearful. "Someone's coming. Listen."

She could hear them, too, and it wasn't just one person. Pairs of feet thudded against the earth floor.

"Which way?" she asked. "Where are they coming from?"

It was almost impossible to tell. The sound echoed, amplified by the close walls of rock and the crossroads they had just passed.

"Run," she said. "Just run!"

"Which way?"

She picked a direction and fled down it, with J hot on her heels. Rémy took them back the way they had come before choosing a different path at the crossroads. They turned a corner and skidded to a halt.

Ahead of them, men were walking single file in

the narrow passageway. They were tall enough to be bent almost double under the rock. The leader saw her immediately, his eyes flashing as he shouted something. They began to run.

Rémy and J rushed back the other way. J stumbled over the rough floor. She picked him up, half-carrying him until he'd found his footing, but it delayed them enough to put their pursuers right on their heels.

She heard a faint cracking sound and then another shout sounded behind her. J fell, tumbling hard against the rock. As she turned to help, Rémy heard another crack and felt something snake around her waist, pulling so tight that it knocked the breath from her body. She was tipped off balance and slammed into the wall before hitting the floor.

The last thing she saw was a sack coming toward her. Something was stuffed into her mouth as the sack was put over her head, blinding her completely. Her hands were bound, and she was hoisted up so that not even her feet touched the ground. Then she was carried off back down the tunnel along which they had just fled.

★ ★ ★

Rémy attempted to struggle against her captors, but it

was useless. She could hear J's angry, muffled yells and was relieved to know that he was at least well enough to protest.

At length, they stopped. She could hear voices talking and then, suddenly, Rémy found herself on a damp floor. Abruptly, the ropes on her wrists were cut and a second later the sack was removed from her head. She spat out the gag, finding a disheveled J beside her.

They were in an altogether darker, danker, smaller underground room than they had seen before. The walls dripped with rust-cultured water and green algae. Rémy scrambled up, the ground slimy under her boots.

They were surrounded by men, all dressed in black. Rémy stood straight, chin high — and then she ran, darting to the left, where she saw an opening.

"J," she shouted. "Go! Run!"

The men were on her in a second — she fought, scratching and biting, but she was no match for them. Fear bit down on her heart — What did they want? What would they do to her? — and made her fight harder.

"Stop," said a voice, as deep and dark as the tunnels around them. "Miss Brunel, please — stop."

She ignored the voice, not wanting to know how the man knew her name. She just needed to get away. And then . . .

"Rémy," she heard someone say, this time in a voice she recognized. "Please, let her go. Let me talk to her! She's just scared, she —"

Rémy was so shocked that she dropped her guard, but the men had already stepped back. The person who had spoken pushed between them to stand in front of her. Rémy stared, open-mouthed.

Chapter 13

CONCEALMENTS

"*You!*"

Before her stood the Professor — Thaddeus Rec's faithful friend, the one who had offered them safe shelter and food.

"I should have known!" Rémy cried, struggling again. "I should have known it was you! No one is ever as kind as you were without wanting something from it."

Rémy saw something flash through the Professor's eyes as his smile disappeared. It was something sharp and angry and — just for a fraction of a second — a little fearful, too. Her mind whirred as she tried to make sense of it all.

"All those different clothes," she went on, still trying to break free. "All that makeup. It was to disguise yourself, wasn't it? To always make yourself look different!"

"Stop," said the Professor, his smile back in place, raising his hands to placate her. "Rémy, please stop. Everything is fine. Let me explain. Everything is —"

"Did Thaddeus know that you have deceived us?" Rémy said. "I hope he did not. I hope, if he still lives, that he never finds out. He thought you were his friend! He thought —"

"I thought what?" Thaddeus asked, as he appeared without warning at the Professor's elbow.

"Mr. Rec!" J shouted, happily. "Well, ain't you a sight for sore eyes!"

"And you, J!" Thaddeus smiled and then turned back to Rémy. "I am so glad to see you both. Are you all right? I'm so sorry . . ."

Rémy blinked for a moment, too stunned to even speak. Then she threw herself at the policeman, her arms around his neck before she even knew what she was doing. Thaddeus stiffened for a moment, before wrapping his arms around her tightly.

"It's all right," he said quietly into her ear. "Rémy, it's all right."

"I was afraid you were dead!" she said, and then, recovering herself, quickly pushed him away. He had a gash over one eye. "What has he done to you?"

Thaddeus touched a hand to his head, as if only just remembering the cut. "Who? Oh — that's nothing. I just hit my head as I fell into the machine. It's fine."

Rémy realized that they were once again surrounded by the Professor's thugs. The man himself was standing close by, as if he had not a care in the world. She pointed at him, her hand shaking with rage.

"This man. This . . . this traitor!" She grabbed Thaddeus's hand and looked around for J. "Thaddeus, together we can fight him and his men. He must be working with Abernathy! We can get away! We can't stay here. You must —"

"Really," said the Professor, "my dear, there is no need for this. You do not understand. There is a perfectly good explanation."

Thaddeus opened his mouth to say something, too, but was stopped by a deep voice, echoing behind her.

"Miss Brunel," it said. "Please do not be afraid."

Rémy turned to see a man taller than any she had ever seen before. His stature was such that he had to stoop under the low ceiling of the tunnel. He looked like a native of the Indian sub-continent, with dark hair and dark eyes set against walnut-hued skin. His head was bound in a richly cultured turban the shade of the deepest sapphires, made to match his robe, which flowed around his sandaled feet. His face was half hidden by a large, dark beard, but his eyes were bright and seemed to hold a smile, though the look on his face was serious.

"I am sorry for your treatment at the hands of my men. They did not mean to harm you, but to merely convey you to safety in the quickest and quietest manner possible. You were in grave danger."

"'Ang on a minute," said J in an awed voice. "I think I know who you are. You're Mr. Desai, ain't'cha? You gotta be. I 'eard of you. I never thought you was real, though."

The Indian man turned to the boy with a smile. "Well, as you see — I am."

"What you doin' down 'ere then? It's a bit . . . I dunno . . . nasty for you, ain't it? Ain't you an Indian prince or somethin'?"

The man called Desai inclined his head, an amused look on his face. "Not exactly, but close enough."

Rémy, confused, looked up at Thaddeus.

"These are Mr. Desai's men, Rémy. They rescued

me. I only got out of that contraption because of them," he explained gently. "Tell her, Professor."

"That is so, indeed, Rémy," said the Professor, stepping forward with a reassuring smile. "They are no more in league with Abernathy than you are. When I realized the tide of the Thames was about to turn and you were still not back, I went looking for help. Now, here I have to confess to some slight subterfuge." The Professor reached out and touched the bottom of Rémy's jacket, at the hole in the hem. "As you slept in the workshop before you all left on your adventure, I secreted one of my devices in this convenient hole." From the tear, he pulled a small, intricate device, something that Rémy did not recognize, but that Thaddeus seemed to have seen before.

"But — Professor, I thought you said the listening device would not work underground," said the policeman, reaching out to take the instrument.

"I was not at all sure it would," the Professor admitted, "and indeed, it ceased to work at all after a short period of time. But it did give me somewhere to start, if only I could find some assistance." He turned to offer a brief bow to Desai, who returned the gesture. "Mr. Desai here was kind enough to provide that. He sent his men after you so that you wouldn't get caught.

When he heard where you were, he was as worried as I was, and evidently with reason."

"Worried! They — they tied me up! They — they," she pointed to her mouth, momentarily forgetting the English word in the midst of her fury, "they gagged me!"

Thaddeus winced. "I'm sorry. That was my fault. I told them you would probably make a lot of noise and fight like the devil."

"You?"

"Well, you did, didn't you?" Thaddeus protested defensively.

"Children, children," soothed Desai's voice. "This is all a tremendous shock, I am sure of it. But we must go. We have other, safer places to be."

Rémy crossed her arms. "I am not going anywhere with you. I do not even know who you are."

Desai inclined his head in an elegant half-bow. "I understand. Please allow me to introduce myself. I am Maandhata Desai, formerly consul to the British East India Company at the city of Hyderabad in Andhra Pradesh, now unfortunate fugitive from both my people and the British government. You must come with us, please. We really are not safe here."

★ ★ ★

Desai and his men led them out of the tunnels and back up to the surface. They found themselves in the crypt of a church, the damp, musty atmosphere barely better than they had experienced underground. Desai walked ahead, up a flight of steep, white stone steps and into the open, empty nave of the church.

A lone figure turned to look at their odd procession as they crossed the vast stone floor. It was the priest, dressed in pale robes that flowed almost as richly as Desai's own. Desai bowed his head as they passed. The priest echoed the gesture in reply, and then turned away, as if deliberately removing them from his sight.

Outside, Rémy was relieved to find that there was a dull light in the sky — it was morning. After being so long in those oppressive tunnels, it was wonderful to be outside again. She breathed in, thankful to be out in the open air at last, even if it was still tainted by the sour smog that always hung over the city.

Beside her, she felt Thaddeus pause. He looked up at the tall, imposing spire of the church. It was so high that it threatened to pierce the rain clouds gathering overhead.

"This is St. Anne's!" he exclaimed in surprise. "We're still in Limehouse!"

"We are," Desai acknowledged. "And that is all the more reason for us to keep moving. Quickly, please. It does none of us any good to be out in the open at the moment, I think."

He took them down to the torpid, greasy waters of Regent's Canal and then walked further east and over a failing wooden bridge into another tangle of streets. Weaving this way and that, they eventually reached a small warehouse that looked as if it had long been abandoned. Its walls were crumbling and overgrown, its high windows cracked and broken. To Rémy, even the roof seemed unsafe.

Inside, though, it was warm and dry — pleasant, even. There was a fire burning in a brick-built hearth in the corner and straw on the floor. Large curtains had been hung in one corner. Desai strode toward them, sweeping them aside to reveal comfortable-looking cushions strewn across a large, patterned carpet.

"Sit, please," Desai ordered, moving his arm expansively. "Make yourselves comfortable. My men will bring us tea."

Rémy looked around to see two of Desai's escort standing guard beside the door. The other two had vanished. She glanced at the Professor. He was looking around as curiously as the rest of them, as if he had never been there before. She didn't know what to make of his sudden appearance underground. Thaddeus obviously still trusted his friend, but there had been that moment when Rémy had seen something unsettling in his eyes.

"Now," said Desai, interrupting her worried thoughts. "Please, sit down. Tell me what three youngsters such as yourselves were doing in such a dangerous place as Abernathy's tunnels. I am all amazement that you even knew they were there."

Rémy looked at Thaddeus, uncertain. He shrugged, and after a moment, she turned back to the Indian. "We were looking for something. Something that we believe Lord Abernathy stole."

Desai inclined his head. "Ah, yes. The Darya-ye Noor, no doubt."

"How do you know that?" Thaddeus asked in surprise.

The man smiled. "Unfortunately for you, Mr. Rec, you have become famous. Look, here."

He threw something to Thaddeus. "A penny paper? Why do you —" He stopped abruptly, staring at the front page of the newspaper.

Rémy leaned over to see what had shocked him into silence. There was a remarkably accurate sketch of

Thaddeus, along with the headline "Fallen Policeman Steals Famed Jewel."

"You see, Mr. Rec," said Desai. "So, now — tell me. Why would you want to steal the Ocean of Light?"

"He didn't!" Rémy blurted out. "Thaddeus didn't — I did! Or . . . or I tried to. He was just . . ."

"In the wrong place, at the wrong time?" Desai asked quietly.

Rémy felt suddenly hot. She stood up, pulling off the jacket the Professor had given her. "I did not mean for him to be blamed. I just had to have the jewel. And now neither of us has it. Abernathy does instead, and . . ."

She trailed off. Desai had gotten to his feet and was staring at her intently.

"What?" Rémy asked. "Why — why do you look at me that way?"

"And how is it that you come to have that?" Desai asked in a low voice, pointing at her throat.

Rémy touched her fingers to her skin, feeling the old chain that always hung around her neck. "This? It is . . . it is an opal, *monsieur*. It is my opal. It belonged to my mother. It is all I have left of my parents."

"Is that so?" Desai asked, moving closer and brushing away her fingers so he could examine the stone. "And who is your mother, that she would give you such a gift? Was she rich? A noblewoman, perhaps?"

Rémy shook her head, mesmerized by his eyes, now staring into hers. "No . . . no, she belonged to the circus, like me. She died when I was very small. My father, too."

"Then how do you know this was a gift from your mother and not a trinket given to you by someone else?"

"I . . . Claudette gave it to me. She told me it was my mother's. She told me my mother wanted me to have it when she died."

"Ah, I see. And do you trust this . . . Claudette?"

Rémy blinked. "She is my oldest friend. She is . . . like a sister. I have no one else. Yes, I trust her. I trust her with my life."

The Indian smiled, a surprisingly gentle gesture that instantly softened his face. "I see. You are lucky to have such a friend. And lucky that you can be so sure of her. Your mother, I suspect, was not so lucky. Not if she was able to give you that."

Rémy stepped away from him. The opal slipped from his fingers, falling once more against her chest. It felt warm. "What do you mean?" she asked. "What do you know about my opal? Gustave said something about it, too. That it had powers I did not know about."

Desai's eyes narrowed and he frowned. "Is that so? And who is Gustave?"

"My . . . my master. At the circus. It was he who wanted me to steal the Darya-ye Noor. He said no other stone would do. He said he had to have it, to break the curse. But he didn't have time to tell me what the curse was, or what he meant about my opal."

"A curse?" Desai repeated. "He said that? He said he needed the Darya-ye Noor because of a curse?"

"Miss Brunel has mentioned this curse before, in fact," observed the Professor. "Though she could not tell us anything more about it."

Rémy suddenly felt very, very tired. She put her hands up to her face, covering her eyes. "I know you will not believe me. But it is the truth. That is what Gustave said."

"Why would I not believe you?"

She dropped her hands. "No one else does. Thaddeus did not."

Rémy glanced toward the young policeman. He was standing a few feet away, listening intently. His cheeks cultured.

"I thought . . ." he began, and stopped. "That was when I thought you were untrustworthy. When I thought . . . when I thought you were just a thieving circus rat. But now . . ."

They stared at each other, confusion and tension bristling between them. Rémy wanted to ask him what he meant. At first he had thought she was nothing but a circus rat, but now? What did he think of her now?

Chapter 14

THE CURSE

*A*bruptly, Thaddeus looked away. Rémy felt her face flush, the confusion of the moment — of everything — piling on her like a landslide.

Desai spoke, his deep voice cutting into the sudden silence like a knife. "Do you know where the Ocean of Light was mined, Miss Brunel?"

She looked back at him, blinking. "Yes, at Golconda, in India. Why?"

Desai stepped forward suddenly, raising his free hand to catch Rémy's chin, holding her still as he examined her face. From the corner of her eye, she saw Thaddeus move quickly, as if he feared Desai were about to hurt her. The Indian must have seen it too, because he glanced at Thaddeus with a brief smile before turning his attention back to Rémy.

"Fear not, young man. I only want to see . . ." he turned her face, gently, this way and that. "Ah, yes. Interesting," Desai said, releasing his hold and stepping back as he gazed once more at the opal.

"What?" Rémy asked. "What do you see in my face? Please, explain."

"You, my dear, are an Indian baby. You may have a French voice, and I have no doubt that your parents were French themselves. But you were conceived in India."

"You cannot possibly know that," Thaddeus protested. "Certainly not from looking at her face!"

"I have to say, that seems rather improbable, Desai," added the Professor. "I'm not sure that science could use a physiognomy to determine place of conception, let alone the naked eye . . ."

Desai shot them both another long-suffering smile. "You may believe what you like, of course. But what I say is true."

"What does it matter?" Rémy asked. "What does it matter where I was conceived?"

Desai nodded. "That is the right question, indeed. It matters because I also know where your opal came from. And together, these things mean that I believe that this curse you speak of is real and dangerous and running within you as it did your parents. So. Would you like to hear more?"

Rémy nodded, her heart thumping painfully. Before this week, she had heard so little about her parents — less than little, really, nothing — that they had seemed insignificant in her life. But now, now that a past she had no idea about was looming so large in her present, it was all she wanted to know about.

Desai insisted that they sit, and so they all did — Rémy, for one, was relieved to finally rest. Once they were settled, Desai began to speak.

"Your opal, Rémy Brunel, was stolen from a very powerful Raja — one of the only true rulers of India left. He was so powerful that not even the French or the British colonists could displace him. They tolerated him, instead. He bided his time and fomented rebellion where he could. It was an uneasy status quo. The colonists could not remove him, and he was not quite strong enough to attack them. I travelled to his court several times on behalf of the British government, and it was a wonder to behold, indeed. His collection of jewels was famed throughout the land, not only for their value and variety but also for their powers."

"Powers?" Thaddeus asked. "What do you mean? Professor, you said something about these powers, too, and I didn't understand you, either. Stones don't have powers. They're just . . . rocks."

The Professor smiled. "Thaddeus, my boy, I am sure that Desai will explain far better than I ever could."

Desai bowed his head, his face growing serious. "For many gems — most, even — it is true that they have no power. But not for all, my young skeptic. A stone may be just a stone, but it took it centuries to become one. Growing slowly beneath the surface, hidden away from prying eyes . . . one cannot pull such an ancient thing from its birthplace and not expect it to bring the wisdom of those ages with it." He pointed to Rémy's opal again. "Take a stone such as this, for example. Some say the colors in an opal are doorways to other places, other worlds. Some say they are angels, trapped by the devil in a fit of rage. Others say that opals are demons in their natural state, which is why they move in their settings."

Rémy touched the gem again. "Gustave said it had powers," she said. "Do you know what he meant?"

"Have you ever been able to hear the thoughts of others?" Desai asked. "In your own head, as if they were your own?"

Rémy shook her head. "No, never. At least, I don't think so."

Desai smiled. "It may yet be sleeping. Stones do, you see. For centuries, sometimes, until they are woken. But even in its slumber, it is a talisman against harm, which is probably why it was given to you in the first place. It was a good choice, too, for it would bestow none of these things upon someone who had stolen it. It must be given willingly and with love, for its powers to work."

Rémy blinked, unsure whether she believed Desai or not. "The curse," she said. "Can you tell me about that? Tell me what happened?"

"I believe that your parents stole a diamond from the same Raja who owned this opal. It was a famed jewel, at that time — as big and as valuable as the Ocean of Light, or even the Mountain of Light."

"And?" Thaddeus asked, apparently as eager to hear as Rémy was herself. "What happened?"

Desai paused as one of his men appeared with a silver tray bearing a tea service and poured a cup for each of them before joining the circle. They all sipped the hot liquid gratefully.

"The story was," Desai went on, "that the Raja welcomed a troupe of performers from Europe into his court, and they stole the gem. They left as soon as the performance was over, intending to head back to their ship and escape. But the theft was discovered almost immediately, and the Raja sent his best men after them. There was a struggle, and the stone was lost forever. It tumbled into the sea at Chinna Ganjam. The Raja was incandescent with rage and ordered his magicians to send a curse after the thieves, their families, and their master. It would only be broken when they returned a stone of equal power, beauty, and worth to the Raja or his descendants."

There was a brief silence as Desai stopped.

"Don't stop there!" J said, evidently enthralled by the tale. "What was it? This curse you said 'e sent after 'em? What'd it do, like?"

Desai paused for a moment and sighed before continuing. "The curses were different, because the Raja perceived that the thieves and their master were different. Their master was greedy and wanted only wealth. So he was cursed to never attain it, no matter how hard he tried. The two thieves . . . it was said they were very much in love with each other. And so their curse was to lose that love and to drive each other away with enmity. The curse continued that their offspring would do the same to those who loved them."

Rémy felt something cold clutch at her heart, but shook her head. "Well, that cannot be me. I am loved, and I love. I love my friend, Claudette, and she loves me. I know she does. And her daughter, Amélie, she may as well be my own. So, I cannot carry the curse you speak of. Can I? It can't have been my parents in your story."

Desai looked at her steadily for a moment before he said, "I do not think that is the kind of love the curse was concerned with, my child."

Rémy tried to laugh. "What other love is there? If you are talking about being in love . . . who would want that, anyway? It is only another burden to carry, another owner to make happy," she shrugged. "And so, if I never am — what does that matter? It sounds like a blessing to me!"

Desai smiled gently. "Be careful what you wish for, Rémy Brunel. If what you have told me is true — about who gave you that opal and who told you to steal the Ocean, then I believe this story must be about your parents. And I have never known a curse like this to turn out as a blessing. It will find a way to wound, unless you break it, which I believe you must."

"This is all just nonsense!" Thaddeus Rec's exasperated voice spoke into the hush that had fallen at

Desai's pronouncement. "All this talk of curses that crush love and powerful jewels — it's all rubbish. And it's not going to help us right now, is it?"

Desai turned to the policeman. "Isn't it?"

"No! What we need to do is sort out this Abernathy business! What he's doing down there in those tunnels is far more important than a stupid gemstone, whether it's got powers or not!"

"I should say so," J piped up. "You didn't see it, Mr. Rec, but 'e 'as got slaves down there, just like everyone's been saying. And I saw Tommy, me mate. We've got to get him out. We've got to get 'em all out!"

"We will, J," said Thaddeus, standing up. "Thank you, Professor, for finding Mr. Desai, and thank you, Mr. Desai, for our rescue. But if you are, as you say, in hiding from the establishment, then this is where we must part ways. Because it is to the establishment I must now go with this information."

"And what information is that, Thaddeus?" the Professor asked.

"Why, the information about what is going on down there, of course, below our feet at this very moment!"

Desai nodded slowly. "You are proposing to tell people, are you?"

"Of course!"

"And then what?" the Indian man asked. "What proof do you have? What evidence is at your disposal to make them listen to you?"

Rémy watched as Thaddeus tried to think of an answer. His shoulders sagged as he realized the truth of Desai's words. He sank down onto the cushions again.

"Your dilemma is mine, too, Mr. Rec," Desai told him. "We have both seen fearful things happening in this city, but we have no one but ourselves to turn to for help."

"I only feel sorry that I have had my head so buried in my own inventions for so long," said the Professor, shaking his head. "To think that there have been such terrible things going on for so long, without me even realizing it."

Rémy frowned, watching the Professor with narrowed eyes. Everyone else around her seemed completely willing to accept the Professor's presence here and his explanation. She wanted to, as well — he was Thaddeus's friend, after all, and the policeman clearly trusted him. And yet . . . she was uneasy. Something didn't feel quite right. She just wasn't sure what it was.

Desai inclined his head. "It is a pity we have not met

before now, Professor," he said. "But I am glad that you have tracked me down. You have provided us all with an exciting opportunity. Perhaps together, with our talents combined, we can prove a force aligned against Abernathy."

"But what is he doing?" Rémy asked. "All those machines down there . . . what are they for? What do they do?"

Desai smiled grimly. "Let me assure you that I know Abernathy of old, and whatever his intentions, they will not be good. His is another name I know from India, a man I have been keeping an eye on ever since I came to England."

"He took the diamond," Rémy said, "the Darya-ye Noor. I know he did."

Desai nodded. "I believe you, Rémy Brunel."

"But — but who is he?" Thaddeus asked, frowning. "Is he really a lord? And if he is, how did he get caught up in all this?"

"Oh yes, he was born a lord," said Desai. "But he aspired to more than the life he had been born to. When I met him, Abernathy had disguised himself and entered the ranks."

"Disguised?" Rémy asked. "How? And why would he do that?"

"It was not as uncommon as you might think," said the Professor, drawing her attention with a smile. "Young men — young women, even — who wanted to explore outside the lives they had been given would hide their true identities in order to enlist. In either the Army or the Navy. I was one of them, in fact."

"You?" Thaddeus asked in astonishment. "You were a military man?"

"Oh, indeed," nodded the Professor. "Though not for as long as I would have liked. Afghanistan, you know. A harsh place. But that, my dear," he added, reaching over and patting Rémy's knee, "is why I can disguise myself, even now. It is an old habit. I just keep thinking of new ways to do it, that's all."

Rémy narrowed her eyes. "But why would you need to disguise yourself to be a recruit? When you could just sign up as yourself?"

The Professor smiled. "Age, my dear. I was too young, and looked it. So, I made myself look older and no one questioned me at all. Once I was inside, no one cared how young I looked as long as I could carry a rifle."

"You never told me," Thaddeus said. "I had no idea!"

The Professor smiled, holding up his empty cup for

Desai's man to refill. "Ah, well — a man must have his secrets, Thaddeus."

Rémy shook her head, frowning. "But what about Abernathy?" she asked Desai. "He was in the army?"

"Yes, he was serving as a British officer," Desai told them. "An engineer, in fact, and a gifted one at that. He was assigned to the court of the same Raja who cursed your parents. I met him there twice and on both occasions our conversation revolved around the Raja's gems and their mystical value. He had, as the British so vulgarly describe it, 'gone native.' He was obsessed with the idea that he could harness the power of the Raja's diamond for his wild engineering ideas. On the night that the diamond was stolen, he joined the Raja's men to chase after the thieves. I distinctly remember thinking at the time that I would not trust him with my most valued possession — and his rage at the stone's loss almost eclipsed that of the Raja himself."

Rémy shook her head. "So . . . so what? You think he has waited all this time, just as Gustave has, to find another stone of equal worth? And he found that in the Darya-ye Noor?"

Desai shook his head. "No. I do not think that is quite what he is looking for. Abernathy is in search of something else."

"What?" Thaddeus asked, his voice irritable. "For goodness' sake, I'm tired of all this double-talk!"

"You mean what 'e's building," J said quietly. "Down there, in the mines. Don't yer, Mr. Desai? That's what yer mean."

"Yes, young man, that is what I mean. That place you found, all those mysterious machines and contraptions you saw? That is a graveyard for all his inventions that have not worked because he could not find a way to power them. He needs a power source. And I think in the Darya-ye Noor, he saw a way to get one. It just so happened that his quest brought him up against you and your master, Rémy." Desai shook his head. "Is it not strange, how often the universe conspires to throw us all together, over and over again?"

"But none of those contraptions were working," said Thaddeus. "Even the cylinder I was in — the fire worked, but inside, it was dead. If what you say is true, wouldn't he be using the power by now?"

"Perhaps he has not perfected the method yet," suggested Desai. "If that is the case, then we still have time to stop him."

Thaddeus shook his head. "But stop him from doing what?"

Desai got to his feet, and they all followed suit. "I

believe that Abernathy is planning to attack London itself," he said, gravely.

"What?" Thaddeus asked, shocked. "Why would he do that? To what end?"

Desai shook his head. "To what end does man ever want power? To dominate, to assert his authority. Who can know for sure? But you have seen what was in that room. Did they seem like peaceful inventions, to you?"

They never got to hear Thaddeus's answer. The air was split by the sudden sound of shouting. The warehouse door was flung open and Rémy turned to see one of Desai's men rush in, flailing his arms and shouting in a language she did not recognize.

"We are found!" Desai shouted. "Quickly, we must flee!"

From outside, there came more shouting, and the sound of heavy boots running closer. Desai lunged toward another door, set in the wall opposite the one they had entered, but before he could reach it, it burst open, the rotten wood splintering on its hinges as men forced their way in.

Rémy turned back to the other door but realized it was too late. More men had entered, pushing Desai's turbaned servants before them. They were all trapped.

She looked up at the broken windows high above, at the curtains hanging from the ceiling. Could she make it up them and through the shattered glass? Should she try? A hand brushed hers, and Rémy lowered her gaze to see Thaddeus watching her.

"If you can make it, go," he whispered.

She found her fingers curling around his, briefly. The sensible thing to do was escape. She knew where the diamond was now, and she knew how to get into Abernathy's tunnels. She could go back. Perhaps she could find it, take it back to Gustave and leave this miserable city for good. Why would she hesitate? Why would she want to?

Rémy pulled away from Thaddeus's touch, swallowing hard. Whatever this pulse in her heart was, whatever it meant, she didn't want it. She was Little Bird, and she flew alone. She didn't need anyone else. She didn't want anyone else. It was feeling like this — torn, tearful — that got you caught. And Rémy Brunel was never caught. At least, not for long.

She turned away from Thaddeus, blinking away tears, and leapt. Rémy caught hold of the heavy curtain and pulled herself up it as if she weighed nothing. She reached the top as shouts from below echoed after her, but she didn't pause to look down. There was a metal pole — an old pipe — that ran along the ceiling, stopping short of the broken window. Rémy gambled that it would take her weight and threw herself toward it, catching it easily.

She was almost at the end when she heard the shot. It was from a pistol — she recognized the tinny double crack as the firing pin hit the bullet and then recoiled. Pain lanced through her. It was only a glancing blow to the arm, but it was enough. Rémy lost her grip and then her only luck was in knowing how to fall. The trick was to relax — to turn your bones to jelly instead of tensing up. That way you were at least less likely to break all of them at once.

She heard Thaddeus's voice, crying her name as she hit the floor. Rémy lay still, unable to move for the pain, winded and who knew what else. She blinked up at her captors, trying to focus. This time she really was in trouble.

Chapter 15

CAPTIVES

"*Rémy!*"

Thaddeus watched as she fell, his ears still ringing with the sound of the gunshot. She hit the ground with a sickening thud, and his eyes blurred. Thaddeus jerked toward her, but before he could take more than a few steps, his way was blocked by a large, stocky man with an angry, scarred face.

"Where do you think you're going, boy?"

Thaddeus looked around. There were more men everywhere, blocking the exits and hustling Desai, his men, and the Professor into a huddle at the center of the warehouse. One had caught J by the neck, and he was struggling, arms and legs flailing helplessly.

Thaddeus looked away, only really thinking of Rémy. She was still lying where she'd fallen, and she wasn't moving. Thaddeus tried to push forward again. "Let me see her! You — you shot her! Let me see," he cried as the man continued to block his path.

The man turned to look over his shoulder, restraining Thaddeus with his hands. As they watched, Rémy began to move. Thaddeus could see her blinking, and relief washed through him. She was alive! She was alive, at least.

"Please," Thaddeus pleaded. "Please — let me see if she's all right."

The man snorted. "Rats like that are always all right. Shame — the streets could do with a clean. Too many dirty foreign whelps on them, if you ask me."

Thaddeus had never felt rage before. He'd always prided himself on being calm, on being the reliable one in a crisis, on solving conflict with reason. But now he was angry, and the fury flooded his veins like the hot burst of a lightning bolt. Before he even knew what he was doing he'd drawn back his arm and thrown a hard punch that caught his captor unawares, just below his ale-fat stomach. The brute was only winded, but it was enough to fold him in half with a dull groan.

Thaddeus dodged him and ran to Rémy. She was still lying on her back, blinking up at the ceiling. Blood was seeping from beneath her. He knelt down beside her and put one hand to her forehead. She was whispering under her breath, words in French that he wouldn't have understood even if he could have fully made them out.

"Rémy?" he asked. "Can you hear me?"

"*Pardonnez-moi avant . . . avant . . . de venir me juger . . .*"

"Rémy? What did you say? I can't . . . can't understand you."

"*Vous ne mépriserez . . . point un coeur . . . contrite . . .*"

Thaddeus heard a bellow behind him that meant his opponent had recovered his voice. He ignored it, moving instead to tear open the arm of her jacket. Beneath it, Rémy's skin was covered in blood, but there was some good news — the bullet wound was only superficial. It had hit her, but it had been a glancing blow.

Rémy coughed and then drew a shuddering breath. "Thaddeus?"

He scrambled back to her side. "Rémy? Are you all right?"

She blinked at him. "*Non.*"

Thaddeus looked her over again. "Tell me where you hurt."

She muttered something in French that may have been an insult, and then said, "Everywhere. I just fell from the ceiling."

"I know, but — no — don't move, not yet!" He put out a hand to stop her as she began to struggle up, a grimace of pain on her face.

"You think I don't know how to fall, policeman?"

Thaddeus opened his mouth, and then shut it again. Then he said, "But you're usually on a wire. Aren't you?"

Rémy gave him a look that could have stripped the hide from a carthorse, but before she could say anything else, Thaddeus felt himself lifted from the floor until only his toes were dragging in the dirt. The strong hands that grasped him belonged to the man he had punched, and he did not look happy.

"You little —"

"Jonesy!" snarled another voice from behind them. Thaddeus could see a thug approaching, his face as dark as thunder.

The man holding Thaddeus turned with a scowl. "What now, Bates?"

"Knock it off," Bates ordered shortly. "Let's get

them down to Abernathy before he starts wondering why we're taking so long, eh?"

Jonesy hesitated for a moment. Then he shook Thaddeus once, hard, and let him go. Thaddeus fell back to the floor and Jonesy lunged forward, pushing his menacing face right into Thaddeus's own.

"I'll be watching you, boy," he said. "You and your little foreign wench."

Thaddeus swallowed his anger and turned back to Rémy, who had torn off more fabric from her trouser leg and was using it to wrap around her wound. He dropped to one knee beside her.

"Are you all right?" she asked, wincing as Thaddeus tied a knot in the makeshift bandage.

"I think I should be asking you that."

"I can look after myself."

"I've noticed."

Rémy smiled at him and then stopped abruptly, turning her face away.

"Right, you lot," barked Bates. "Let's get moving, shall we? Lord Abernathy wants to know why you dropped by his place without so much as stopping for a cup of tea."

★ ★ ★

Rémy let Thaddeus help her up, but only because she had to. The fall had hurt her more than she was willing to let on, and she was fairly sure she'd cracked a rib or two. Still, she'd been lucky. Rémy knew it could have been much worse — probably should have been, in fact. She touched the opal at her throat. It was a talisman against harm, Desai had said. Maybe it really was. But then, if he'd been right about that . . . it meant he was right about the curse, too.

Rémy almost fell as one of Abernathy's men jabbed her in the back, urging them to move faster. Thaddeus caught her, his arm slipping around her easily. She realized she liked the feel of it there and then stamped on the thought, squashing the life out of it before it had time to take root. He was a policeman; she was a thief. They wanted the same jewel but for vastly different reasons. She just had to remember what she was there for, that was all.

Abernathy's men took them back into the tunnels but not via the crypt this time. Outside, it had begun to rain again. The day was giving way to a grimy evening, darkness falling amid a pall of gritty smog. The men herded them like cattle, several ahead and several behind. People who passed turned their heads away and scuttled faster, anxious not to be drawn into trouble. The downcast group was forced to walk back down to the canal path, but instead of heading to Limehouse, they stopped beneath one of the bridges.

At first Rémy thought that the men intended to drown them in the oily water — that the talk of Abernathy had merely been a ruse. She half-turned to Thaddeus, intending to tell him to run. But instead of death, they were offered darkness.

The leader opened a narrow wooden door, hidden in the side of the bridge. There was a steep flight of steps that led down into the blackness. The Professor was pushed in first, followed by Desai. Rémy watched as J was then shoved forward. She saw him darting small, furtive looks this way and that, which told her he was planning something. She tensed instinctively, waiting for what was to come and willing him to succeed.

A split second later, J made a break for freedom. He ducked out of his captor's grasp and made a run for the grassy bank that led up to the road above. Abernathy's men were too fast, even for J. One of them shouted a warning, and two of them dashed after him. One grabbed at his arm and missed, but the other got a grip on his ankle and wrenched him back.

J yelled as he flew through the air, crashing onto the hard pebble track of the canal path and curling up like a beetle.

"He's just a boy!" Rémy shouted, cursing at them. "A child! Leave him alone!"

The men ignored her, scooping J up and planting him, tearful, back on his feet before pushing him roughly through the dark doorway and down the stairs.

"You two," said Jonesy, "get yourselves down them steps, or I'll throw you down 'em. Understand?"

Rémy glanced at Thaddeus before moving forward. At the top of the steps, she looked down. They spiraled steeply into darkness, though there was a light flickering somewhere below. She reached out to grasp the thin wooden handrail, flinching slightly. Her arm was stiff, the muscles around the gunshot wound clenched with the pain, and the rest of her felt as if she'd been crunched through a mangle at least once. Before she could begin the descent, she felt Thaddeus's hand on her shoulder.

"I don't want you to fall again," he said. "Let me carry you."

"Pfft," she replied. "When I am in my coffin, then you can carry me."

"Don't say things like that."

Rémy started down the steps with him close behind. "Why do you care?" she asked. "You know what I am. A thief. So why do you care?"

Thaddeus said nothing, and she glanced back up at him. His face was cloaked in shadow, but his mismatched eyes caught the meager light from below. He was not looking at her, and she noticed he was frowning. He looked deep in thought and she wondered why, and then decided that she didn't want to know.

Rémy turned away and moved more quickly, ignoring the tearing pain that bit into her arm. They reached the bottom and found themselves back in the narrow, close-formed tunnels from which they had escaped not so long ago. Their captors hustled them along until the tunnel they were in opened out into a wider room. Alcoves had been carved into the dank walls, closed off by heavy, metal bars spaced several inches apart. They were clearly cells.

The men divided the group in two and pushed them into opposite cells — Desai's men in one, and the rest of them in the other. All except J.

"Not you," growled the man called Jonesy, as J went to follow Thaddeus and Rémy into the cell. "We've got other plans for you."

Rémy watched as J looked up at the big man fearfully. "What ya' goin' to do to me, mister?"

Jonesy grinned — a cruel, cold expression that darkened his eyes. Bending down until his face was level with the boy's, he said, "You're going to do the first honest day's work of your life, son."

J flinched and Rémy thought he was going to make another run for it, but Jonesy was way ahead of him. He nipped J's ear between his fat fingers, pinching until the boy yelped in pain, and still the thug did not let go, the grin on his face widening.

Rémy threw herself at the bars. *"Lâche!"* She shouted, enraged, "Ugly, useless coward, to bully a child! You —"

Jonesy lunged at the bars and, without letting go of J, reached through to wrap his thick hand around her slim throat. She choked, struggling to breathe, but Jonesy only gripped harder. He shook her like a dog shakes a rat caught in its jaws. She heard Desai and Thaddeus shouting, but the sound seemed to be coming from a very long way away. Darkness flickered at the edges of her vision and then, beyond its jagged edges, she saw a light brighter than she'd ever seen before. Rémy thought she sensed Death riding upon it, coming for her, and she realized that actually, she wasn't as scared as she might have been. Life hadn't proven so easy, after all. Death couldn't be much harder, could it?

She felt herself falling.

Chapter 16

REVELATIONS

$\mathcal{T}$haddeus caught Rémy before she hit the floor and held her limp body on his lap. Abernathy's men disappeared into the tunnels, laughing and chattering.

"Is she dead?" he asked, the horror of his question engulfing him like a pit. "Is she dead?"

Desai knelt beside them, gently pulling one of Rémy's eyelids back and then shaking his head. "No. She is unconscious. She will be fine."

The Indian man fumbled beneath his robes for a moment before pulling out a vial of red liquid. "We must give her this. It will revive her and kill her pain, at least for a time."

Thaddeus held her closer. "What is it?"

"The essence of a plant found in my country, that is all."

"Opium?" Thaddeus asked. "Because I've seen what the poppy does, and you're not giving her that."

Desai shook his head. "Not opium. Far rarer than that. It is harmless, I assure you. Please. Let me help her."

Thaddeus nodded, still reluctant but with no alternative. Desai smoothed Rémy's hair back from her pale face and then tipped the vial, pouring a few drops of liquid between her lips. Nothing happened for a moment, and then she coughed, her limbs jerking back into life as she gasped for air. Desai stepped back.

"It's all right," Thaddeus told her, as she opened her eyes. "You're all right."

To his surprise she curled into him, drawing her knees up and leaning her head against his chest. He wrapped his arms around her, relieved to feel her breathing normally.

"I have got to stop trying to get myself killed," she muttered, the quiet words fluttering against his throat.

Her comment made him laugh. "You have, indeed. There are cats with fewer lives than you."

Rémy shuddered and then pulled away from him to look him in the eye for a moment. She seemed to be searching for something there, but he didn't know what she was looking for. Her eyes were clear and bright, and the thought that the day would come when he would no longer see them filled Thaddeus with a sudden flash of despair.

Rémy blinked, a frown crossing her face. She pulled away from him, shrugging off his offer to help her to her feet. Stretching out her arm, she pointed her fingers as if she were balancing on the high wire.

"Every circus performer would take a vial of your medicine a day, *monsieur*, if they knew it existed," she said, looking at Desai.

Desai inclined his head in his customary half-bow. "It is a useful concoction."

She nodded. "Do you have anything to melt metal bars? Because that would also be useful at this moment."

"Sadly," said Desai, pocketing the vial and what was left of the medicine inside it, "that vial is in my other robe."

Thaddeus went to the bars and shook them, but they were solid. Opposite, he could see Desai's men doing the same, to no avail. The bars seemed stronger even than iron — they were silver, like that cursed machine that had held him captive only hours before.

"Professor?" he asked, turning to his friend, who had sat huddled and silent in one corner since their incarceration. "Do you know what this metal is?"

The Professor looked up unhappily. His face was gray and ashen. He blinked slowly at Thaddeus's question and then said, "It is titanium. It is very, very strong — and very light, too. Excellent stuff."

"Titanium?" Thaddeus asked. "But . . . but isn't that a chemical element? Not a metal, surely?"

His friend stood up slowly. "There have always been theories, ever since its discovery, that it could be prepared as a metal," he said.

Thaddeus looked at the bars again. "Do you — do you mean that Abernathy has managed to do it?"

The Professor moved to stand beside Thaddeus, lifting a finger to run it smoothly down the silver metal. "Yes, Thaddeus. Him, or someone working for him . . ." his voice trailed off.

"Do you know a way to break it?" Desai asked, coming to stand beside them, too. "In theory, if not in practice?"

The Professor shook his head. "Sadly, I do not. Titanium is incredibly strong, stronger than any other metal ever mined, discovered, or produced. That is why it is so valuable and its metallurgy so fascinating."

Thaddeus turned to survey the rest of their surroundings and caught sight of Rémy watching the Professor with narrowed eyes. He wondered what she was thinking.

* * *

As Rémy watched the Professor, she was, indeed, deep in thought, her earlier suspicions flooding back. Her pondering was disturbed by the sound of footsteps, hard against the compacted earth of the tunnel. A greater light grew nearer — gas, this time, rather than the poor candle they had been left with. A figure hove into view, striding ahead of his men, upright and strong — a leader — Lord Abernathy, himself.

He was tall — not as tall as Desai, but not far off. His body lithe and lean. Rémy looked for a trace of the old man she'd had the misfortune to meet at the Tower of London, but she could find none. Could this really be the same man? Surely not. He looked strong — not young, but not more than fifty, and he carried the years well. His face was thin, with a long jaw that tapered beneath a pronounced aquiline nose. His eyes were large, with hooded lids over blue irises. Abernathy was dressed in a well-cut suit of the finest cloth. A pocket watch hung from his breast pocket, shining silver in the gaslight. A red cravat was tied at his neck against a starched, perfectly white shirt.

His party came to a halt before the bars, and one of his men stepped forward to unlock the door.

"Lord Abernathy," he announced, as his master stepped inside.

Rémy was still staring in silence, trying to fathom how this could be the same man who had tricked her out of the Darya-ye Noor, when Thaddeus spoke.

"You are not Lord Abernathy," he said, his voice incredulous. "I have met Lord Abernathy — he is a frail gentleman. Whoever you are, sir, you are an imposter."

The man narrowed his eyes for a moment, staring at the policeman. Then without warning, he threw back his head and laughed. It was a high, thin sound that bounced from the walls and echoed around the labyrinth of tunnels.

"Oh, my dear boy," he said, once he had wiped the tears from his eyes. "Never let it be said that Scotland Yard isn't the finest detective force in all the world. And how thankful I am for that."

"You may laugh, *monsieur*," interjected Rémy, feeling compelled to defend Thaddeus, "but I have met Abernathy, too, and you are not he."

The suited man turned his gaze upon her, one eyebrow raised. "Ah, yes. Rémy Brunel. Indeed, we have met. But do you not recognize me?"

He leaned forward a little, his shoulders dipping toward her and his eyes holding hers. She stared into those eyes . . . and, yes, there was that bright twinkle, the one she had seen on the night when it all went wrong. The rheumy eyes had given way to more youthful ones, but there was no mistaking their intelligence. Rémy gasped, taking a step back.

"It is you! But how?"

Abernathy turned away with a wave of one elegant hand. "My dear girl, as a trickster yourself, I am surprised you need to ask."

Rémy heard an intake of breath — it came from Thaddeus. "You charlatan!" he accused. "And I suppose now you will tell us that you did take it? That it was you who stole the jewel from the Tower."

Abernathy's blue eyes regarded Thaddeus coolly. "I wouldn't worry about the diamond if I were you, Thaddeus Rec. You have more pressing concerns at hand," he said before turning his back again. He stepped in front of Desai. "As for you, Desai, I heard you were in London. I have been searching for you for a long time. I felt sure you had come for me."

Desai inclined his head, a grim look on his face. "I did not know it at the time, but it seems perhaps I did. I always knew we would meet again."

Abernathy snorted. "Is that so? Then I am surprised you did not also know that it would be very bad for you if we did."

Abernathy spun suddenly to confront the Professor. "Aha!" he exclaimed. "And my dear Professor, how long has it been? Let's see . . . at least a month, I think? Too long, in truth!"

Rémy felt Thaddeus tense beside her as he realized that his friend and this villain knew each other. She swallowed hard, hoping for his sake that her worst fears were not about to be realized.

"Professor?" Thaddeus asked in a hushed voice, before falling silent again.

Abernathy held up a hand in Thaddeus's direction, commanding silence. He leaned in toward the other man. "Imagine my surprise, my old friend," he said with quiet menace, "to discover that you were one of those who came into my realm unbidden. That perhaps you even led these trespassers into it. Hmm?"

The Professor began to reply, but Abernathy cut him off with a flick of his wrist. "But no matter. The plan is almost complete. Soon I will put it into action, this wonderful vision that you helped me to realize, Professor. And then no one will stand in my way. Certainly not you, Desai," Abernathy spat, turning to the Indian, "or this ragamuffin band of outcasts and foreigners."

"Where is the stone?" Rémy interrupted. "The Ocean of Light. Is it here? What have you done with it?"

Abernathy turned to look at her with disdain. "My goodness. I was aware that circus folk were people of little intelligence, but surely, girl, even you must know when the game is up — or rather, when it has turned to more lofty goals."

Rémy shook her head. "I just want to know, *monsieur.*"

Abernathy was dismissive. "Simply accept that you were beaten at your own game and be done with the matter." He turned back to the Professor.

"That I cannot do," she said, to his back. "I need it. To break a curse."

Abernathy froze.

"Don't you recognize her name, Abernathy?" Desai's deep voice broke into the sudden silence. "You should. You complained about it often enough, all those years ago."

The Lord turned slowly on his heel before stepping closer.

"Brunel," he said.

"Yes, *monsieur.*"

His eyes pierced her. "Brunel. My God, I should have known. Your parents —"

"Stole a diamond. I know. And now I am cursed and I will stay cursed, until I replace it."

Abernathy's fascination turned to glee. He slapped his tailored thigh and laughed his high, thin laugh. "How wonderful! After all these years! And what a coincidence!"

"Coincidence, Abernathy?" said Desai. "No. It is fate."

Abernathy snorted in derision. "Fate? Well, if that's true, then fate has something terrible in store for you, my friend. You're as meddling as you were sixteen years ago, and trust me — this time nothing will stand in my way."

Then without warning, Abernathy drew a pistol and fired a shot at the Indian. The bullet struck him full in the chest. A bright flower bloomed red in the midnight of his robe as he staggered backward against the bars before slumping to the floor. From the cell opposite came a collective roar as Desai's loyal men saw their leader dying before them. They ran at the bars, shaking them so hard that it seemed sure they would be dislodged.

Abernathy waved his arm. "Get rid of them," he snarled. "Put them in harness and make them work or something. For goodness' sake, what a racket."

His orders were followed immediately, his thugs dragging Desai's men away down the stone passageway, their anger echoing against the walls as they struggled in vain. Amid the noise, Rémy rushed to Desai. She knelt beside him, hearing his erratic breathing. The bullet seemed to have hit him full in the chest — surely nothing could save him from such a direct shot? He was mouthing words, his eyes shut, and she wondered if he was praying to whatever god he worshipped. Rémy leaned forward and Desai's dark eyes opened and fixed on hers. He shook his head and his mouth moved as if he wanted to tell her something, but he was already too weak.

Desai's eyes fluttered closed again as the life seemed to leave his body. Rémy sat back on her heels, shocked by the abruptness of his death. One moment he had been helping her, and the next . . .

She stood up to find Thaddeus standing between her and Abernathy, as if to shield her from his gun.

Something rushed through her, catching her heart and making it flutter on wings she did not know it possessed. But then came something else that doused that unexpected flicker of joy with stark, cold fury. It threatened annoyance, exasperation even, at Thaddeus's determination to protect her. She didn't need his help. She didn't need anyone, especially not a straight-laced policeman. She could get herself out of this mess and hang everyone else. She pushed past him roughly, moving to stand nose-to-nose with Abernathy.

"What is it?" she asked. "Your plan? Why are you doing this? Enslaving people? Killing people? To what end?"

Abernathy grinned at her, and in his cold, blue eyes, she saw pure arrogance and a flash of something that she had only see once before — in the face of a madman.

"Sorry," he said, "but that's information only my closest advisors are privy to. Advisors such as the Professor, here," Abernathy stepped away from her and up to the man Thaddeus had trusted implicitly. "Come now, Professor. Your last chance, you know. I can still use a man like you."

The Professor hesitated for a moment, turning toward Thaddeus. "Thaddeus," he began, and then he seemed to change his mind. He gave a small shrug of his shoulders instead and moved toward the cell door.

"Marvelous! Then let us away, out of this nasty, damp place. We have work to do, kinks to iron out . . ."

Before Abernathy reached the door, he stopped suddenly. He stood still, with his back to them for a moment, and then turned slowly to face them, his gaze fixed on Rémy.

"But wait . . ." he said. "Something has occurred to me."

"Whatever it is," Thaddeus said coldly, "we don't want to hear it."

Abernathy waved his hand. "I have no interest in you, boy. A second-rate policeman is of no use to me. But you . . ." He pointed at Rémy. "You are altogether different."

Rémy had no idea what he was talking about. She stepped back as Abernathy edged slowly toward her, wary of what he was about to do.

"You could be helpful to me," he said, his voice sly and low.

She was conscious of Thaddeus standing nearby, watching her with wide eyes. Annoyance flooded through her again, and she lifted her chin, defiant.

"Oh?" she asked. "And how is that?"

"I could use someone like you. Someone . . . quick and agile. I very much enjoyed watching your display at the Tower of London, and I must admit I was impressed that you made it onto the roof."

Rémy sensed Thaddeus stiffen as she remembered how close he had come to catching her that night. She wondered where she would be right now if he had.

"Rémy," Thaddeus said quietly, his voice unsure.

"Join me. You could be very useful . . . Little Bird."

Rémy blinked, trying not to reveal her surprise. From the corner of her eye she saw Thaddeus clench his hands and shake his head, but she ignored him.

"Why would I do that?" she asked Abernathy instead. "What would be in it — for me?"

Abernathy laughed his high, shrill laugh again. "Well," he said. "You'd have to join me to find out, my lady Brunel. Join me or stay locked away down here in this cell with your dead friend and a useless policeman. I know you need the Ocean of Light. I was there when your parents were cursed, remember? And who knows? One day I may no longer have need of it. If you were to show yourself worthy . . ." He stepped away with a brief grin and a small shrug. "It is your choice, of course. But make it quickly."

Rémy deliberated. Join Abernathy? It seemed

preposterous, but as she thought about it, the idea became more and more appealing. It would get her out of this prison, after all, and give her a chance to find out where the diamond was being held.

She felt Thaddeus's eyes on her and met his anxious gaze. "Don't," he said. "I — Rémy, don't. He's a villain. And you — you have a good heart. I know you do. I trust you, Rémy Brunel. Don't even think about doing this."

Rémy held his gaze. So, he trusted her. He thought she had a good heart. But now he believed she was genuinely considering joining Abernathy's side. He thought she might turn. The realization made her angry, and she looked away from him. All she wanted was the stone, and she knew she must do anything necessary to get it. Of course, if she stayed with Thaddeus Rec, he'd do everything he could to make sure she didn't.

Chapter 17

THE TRUTH
WILL OUT

$\mathcal{R}$émy nodded. *"D'accord,"* she told Abernathy. "Let's go. Get me out of here."

"Rémy," she heard Thaddeus say.

"You'll be safe here, little policeman," she responded without looking at him. "You can't get into any trouble here."

"For God's sake!" Thaddeus stepped in front of Rémy before she could follow Abernathy out of the cell, forcing her to look at him. "You can't help him."

Rémy narrowed her eyes. "Why not? We don't even know what he's doing yet. It may turn out to be something good."

Thaddeus laughed in disbelief. "He's kidnapping

people! He's keeping them as slaves! Whatever he's doing, he's doing it with slave labor."

Rémy stuck out her chin. "Plenty of things we now think are wonderful were built by slaves, Thaddeus. Or have you forgotten that?"

"That's not the p—"

"Miss Brunel!" Abernathy's voice thundered from the tunnel outside. "Come now, or I lock you in."

Rémy shrugged. "I must go."

"Don't," said Thaddeus, catching her uninjured arm. "Please. Why are you doing this? This isn't you, I know it isn't."

Rémy shrugged him off as she headed after Abernathy. "How can you possibly know that?" she asked over her shoulder. "You haven't even known me a week of days. By the turn of the new moon, you will have forgotten me."

One of Abernathy's men clanged the cell door shut behind her. She stopped and looked back, just for a moment. Thaddeus stood on the other side of the door, gripping the bars. Behind him, Desai's body still lay in the dirt where he had perished.

"I won't," he said as she turned to leave. "I won't forget you, Rémy Brunel. I wouldn't. I can't. Stay here. With me. Please."

Rémy paused again. She remembered the first time she had seen him, looking up at her from the sawdust into which he'd fallen after he tried to save her. And here he was, trying to save her yet again — but this time, from herself.

"Stop trying to rescue me, Thaddeus Rec," she said. "We are what we are. I am a thief. You are a policeman. I steal, and you try to stop me. You are on the right side of the law, and I will always be outside it. That's all. Don't pretend that we are more than we are. We never were. We never will be."

"Last chance, Miss Brunel." Rémy looked up to see Abernathy a little way along the passage with the Professor. "I am not a patient man."

"I'm coming," she said. As she walked away, she could feel Thaddeus's eyes on her until the stone corridor finally kinked and saved her from his gaze.

* * *

As Thaddeus watched Rémy go, his heart turned to lead. How could she do it? How could she leave him here alone, to put herself in league with a murderer?

As she and his captors disappeared from sight, Thaddeus turned away from the bars and let himself sink to the ground. He shouldn't be surprised by

Rémy's change of heart, he knew that. She'd said it herself — they hadn't even known each other a week, and they were so different. Their lives were so different. Rémy seemed to accept that she was a thief. Part of him thought she even enjoyed it. Whereas he, on the other hand, could not bear the thought of owning something he had not honestly earned. They were chalk and cheese as Mrs. Carmichael, his landlady, would surely say. Too different to live peaceably, that was for sure. And yet, this . . . He had thought she was better than this. And he'd hoped . . .

Thaddeus rubbed a hand over his face, shaking the thought away. There was no point. She was gone, and he was on his own in a cell with little hope of rescue. He looked at Desai's body, still lying where he had died such a senseless, ignominious death. The nobleman's face was uncovered still, his arms lying limp by his sides in the dirt.

Thaddeus pulled himself to his feet and walked over to the dead man. Intending to give Desai at least a little dignity, he went to pull the Indian's robe up over his face.

A movement caught Thaddeus's eye. He stared for a moment and then shook himself. Desai was dead — of course he hadn't moved. Thaddeus took hold of the robe again and was about to lay it over Desai's face when the dead man drew a great, shuddering, stuttering breath — an unexpected gasp for air. Thaddeus started in shock, dropping the cloth in his hands as Desai coughed and struggled to open his eyelids.

"Desai?" Thaddeus asked, rapidly getting over his fright. He placed one hand on the man's shoulder, the other on his warm cheek. "My God — you're alive!"

Desai blinked up at Thaddeus, his eyes clouded. "So . . ." he managed weakly, "so . . . it would appear."

Thaddeus fumbled at the man's chest, where the bullet had torn through his robes. There was a hole, proving that there had definitely been a bullet. Thaddeus pulled his hand away. It was smeared red, but as he held it up in the dim light, he realized something.

"This isn't blood! Desai . . ."

Desai struggled to move and Thaddeus supported him until he was sitting upright, his back leaning against the cell bars. He touched his hand to his chest with a frown, and then pulled apart his robes to reveal the bare skin beneath. Something tinkled faintly among the folds as he pushed aside the material and, a moment later, Desai pulled out several tiny shards of glass.

"The vial," he muttered. "It must have been hit."

Thaddeus shook his head. "But what happened to the bullet? It cannot have hit you. Maybe — maybe, somehow, the cloth was enough to stop it."

Desai shook his head, rearranging his robes and coughing again. "It hit me," he said. "I felt it, right here." He pointed to his chest, just above his heart.

"Then — how?"

Desai shut his eyes again, shaking his head. "It must have been the contents of the vial. The concoction is a very old remedy and very strong. The Pashtuns used to smear it on their bodies before going out to face your British rifles. I have never seen it cheat death before, but . . ." he shrugged, opening his eyes again. "It is not generally used in such concentrated doses."

Thaddeus nodded, still unable to quite take it all in. "I can't believe it," he said. "You're not dead. You should be dead, but . . . you're not dead!"

Desai offered a wan smile. "If it is any consolation," he said, "I do not feel at all well."

"Is there anything I can do?"

Desai shook his head and then looked around slowly. "We are alone?"

Thaddeus sat back against the bars beside Desai, resting his arms on his drawn-up knees. "Yes."

"They both followed him? The Professor and Rémy Brunel?"

Thaddeus swallowed, annoyed to feel the lump that had risen in his throat. "Yes. Both of them."

Desai reached out to place a trembling hand on Thaddeus's shoulder. "I am sorry, my friend. I should have suspected the Professor, but I confess, I did not."

Thaddeus's eyes blurred, and he looked down at the floor, unable to speak.

"As for Rémy Brunel — please remember the curse before you think too badly of her."

"The curse?" Thaddeus croaked. "What do you mean?"

"Were you not listening when I explained it?" Desai asked. "She carries it, the same as her parents. She is destined to drive away the one she loves. I saw it already beginning to work, even before I had explained it to her. She is a victim as much as you and I, Thaddeus, and her actions may not be of her own volition. However, I have hope. She is a strong girl, in both body and mind. I think you may find she has a plan all of her own to which you were not privy."

Thaddeus stared at the floor, trying to follow all that Desai had told him. But his mind kept getting caught on one detail.

"Wait," he said. "Wait — you said that the curse would be activated when . . . when . . ."

"When she fell in love, yes. Her parents were already very much in love, of course, with each other. But in Rémy's case . . ."

Thaddeus interrupted, frowning. "So, if the curse has been activated now, surely that means . . . that means . . ."

Desai smiled. "Yes?"

Thaddeus shook his head. His heart was turning over painfully. "No. It's nothing. It doesn't matter. Forget I brought it up."

Desai laughed softly, shaking his head. "Ah, to be young again, with all the agony it brings."

Thaddeus felt his cheeks reddening, and cleared his throat. "Are you feeling well enough to stand?"

"I believe I might be," said Desai, evidently still amused.

"Good," said Thaddeus, getting sharply to his feet. "Because there must be some way out of this cell. I suggest we look for it."

★ ★ ★

Rémy followed Lord Abernathy and the Professor through the winding corridors of earth and rock. She tried to make out whether any of the places they were walking now were paths she had trodden before, but for her at least, it was impossible to tell. At one point, they reached a fork in the tunnels, and from deep within one, she could hear the relentless clanging from Abernathy's slave mine. Most of Abernathy's men left them here — they bowed deeply to their master and disappeared, one by one, down the corridor that led to the mine. Rémy thought about J and felt a jolt of anxiety laced with guilt. But there was nothing she could do to help him. Not right now, anyway.

"Come now, Miss Brunel, no daydreaming," called Abernathy. Rémy realized that they had walked ahead and left her standing, thinking about her friend. "There is nothing of interest in this part of the labyrinth, my dear."

She hurried to catch up, as Abernathy led them on still farther. The tunnel they were in banked suddenly, curving to the right and then — to Rémy's surprise — widening out and ending abruptly in a flight of steps. Two more huge guards were standing either side of the tunnel, dressed in something resembling a uniform — trousers and loose shirts, both cut from a cloth of deep red and held in place by a wide cummerbund. Their clothes made Rémy think of Desai's flowing robes. But what really caught her attention were the glittering, curved blades of their drawn swords.

"At ease, at ease," Abernathy told them affably, as the small group neared and then drew to a halt. "All is well, as you can see."

The two men bowed deeply, re-sheathing their weapons. "Lord Abernathy."

He nodded to them in return, sweeping between them and down the steps, which here were carved straight out of the compacted earth. Ahead of them was another short passageway, lit by flickering gas lamps that hung on the walls. This tunnel ended in a wall of rock into which had been fitted a narrow wooden door. Rémy could hear distant, echoing noises from beyond it. Men shouting, heavy objects being moved — the busy whir and conference of industry.

Abernathy strode to the door and flung it open, stepping out onto the wooden platform that lay beyond. "And see here, Miss Brunel — behold, the future, right here."

Abernathy moved his arm in an expansive gesture, sweeping it out around him as if he were showing her the world. Rémy stepped forward onto the wooden parapet, and her mouth fell open in amazement.

They were standing above another cavern like the

one she, Thaddeus, and J had first found themselves in after their journey through the sewer. But this one was twice as large. And what lay within was many times more astonishing. Gaping around her, Rémy was stunned into silence.

Everywhere she looked was a new wonder to behold. Largest of all of them were four silver vessels that looked to be related to the one they had seen in that first room they had emerged into from the sewer — was it only days ago? It seemed like years, so much had happened in between. They looked like boats, ships almost, their hulls hammered smooth enough to shine, their bows sharpened to vicious points that glinted in the harsh light. At the stern of each was a huge mechanical contraption that resembled the spokes of a wheel without the outer ring and a sloped walkway that could evidently be sealed up for travel, but for now lay open. The upper decks were encased in domes of glass, clear enough for Rémy to see through. She observed several men, all moving purposefully, carrying boxes, barrels, and bags this way and that within the enclosed space of the ship. They were dressed in the same uniforms of red that she had seen on the two guards, and they all bore the same forbidding-looking swords.

The ships stood not on the dirt floor, but supported on huge wooden struts that were built from the whole trunks of trees, strong enough to take their weight. Between each vessel was a wooden walkway, with steps leading down to the ground and up to a platform that ran around the edge of the room. There were two entrances onto the platform — one on which Rémy now stood and one directly opposite on the other side of the cavern.

The ships were not the only items of wonder. Below them, filling almost every spare inch of the cavern's base, were more of the suits she had seen. But as with the ships, these suits were streamlined — clearly a better version. Though still metal, they seemed to be jointed in more places, allowing for easier movement. Besides the glass helmet, they also had tanks attached to their backs, as if for carrying water. Since the suit was completely enclosed, however, Rémy wondered whether they might be for carrying air, instead. Standing beside the rows of metal suits was something else, too — racks of something more recognizable, though still strange. Rifles — hundreds of them — all equipped with the cruel spike of a bayonet, but also a strange glass bulb of purple gas. Alongside them were more swords.

"Your silence does you credit, Miss Brunel," said Abernathy. "In truth, it is a sight too wondrous for words, is it not?"

Rémy blinked. She realized that what she was feeling was not wonder but fear. In all the amazing sights below her, she could see no peaceful use for these machines. Instead, it seemed clear to her that Abernathy was preparing for war. The suits were lined up like an army and, in truth, why else would he need such a wealth of weaponry?

"Extraordinary, indeed," she said.

"Ah, but my dear young lady, you have not seen the best of it yet!"

Lord Abernathy stepped to the edge of the parapet and leaned over the railing. He called down to one of the uniformed men in a language Rémy did not understand. The man below nodded and bowed, running immediately to one of the machines. There was a short delay and then, suddenly, a panel slid open in the side of the vessel. There was a clattering sound, and Rémy could see a wooden structure unfurling from the open space, growing as it did so, into a cloth-covered wing. She stared at it.

"These . . . surely they do not fly?"

Abernathy laughed in glee at her shock, slapping his

hand down on the wooden railing. "As I said — wondrous, is it not? We have not tested them in the air but the Professor here has never been wrong yet."

"And these are all a part of your plan, my Lord?"

"Hmm? Oh, yes, yes, my dear, of course. Although it has to be said that for Phase One, we will not be requiring the wings." He turned and waved his arm in a curt gesture. Aboard the vessel, the wing began to retract once more. "For now, all we need is the ships' underwater capabilities."

Rémy shifted from one foot to the other. Her stomach was beginning to turn over in fear. "Underwater capabilities?"

"Yes, indeed. They can sail beneath the water, not simply on top of it. Amazing, are they not?"

"But — why would you want them to do that, my Lord?"

Abernathy smiled at her. "London is a city of rivers, Miss Brunel. They run everywhere, where we see them and where we don't. The Thames is only the trunk — the roots spread far and wide beneath the city, just as these tunnels do here. But for some reason, no one has ever thought to navigate them."

Rémy frowned. "And — and you intend to? But why?"

"Is it not obvious?" Abernathy asked. "Because no one expects an attack from below. In fact, these men will not expect an attack at all, which is what makes it all so very perfect. And then we will rise out of the waters of the Thames, right beneath every center of power. We will take them by surprise — and as you know yourself, my dear Rémy Brunel — the element of surprise is worth an entire army of men."

Rémy's heart thumped against her rib cage. "But — you are going to attack the city? Why?"

Abernathy tutted. "Not the city, my dear. The government. That indolent rabble who are letting the greatest empire in history slide through their fingers. The 'Scramble for Africa!' What fools, to take our attentions toward such an uncivilized continent. They should be looking east, expanding further in India and beyond into Asia — as far as China, even. I offered them the means to become the power to be reckoned with on Earth for a thousand years or more . . . but they refused it. Well, so be it. If they will not willingly accept my power, I will have to force it upon them. And, my God, how I will make them regret their pompous pigheadedness!"

Rémy had nothing to say in answer to this tirade. She stared out at the wonder beneath her and felt her sweat turn cold as fear seeped into her veins. He would do it, she knew he would. She could hear the insanity in Abernathy's words, in his absolute conviction that he was right and not only that, but that he would succeed. He would attack the British Empire right at its heart. It sounded ridiculous — except that Abernathy had all this at his fingertips and no one who mattered knew about it. It was all here, hidden right under the city. Right beneath London.

"Well, Miss Brunel. As you know — because I am sure that Desai explained it — I have in my possession the final piece of the puzzle. The diamond that you so valiantly tried to steal will finally allow me to set my plan in motion. Which, incidentally, I think must happen a little sooner than I thought, Professor," he said, addressing the silent man at Rémy's side. "We have attracted a little more attention from the outside than I would have liked. Which, quite frankly, I have you to thank for, don't I?"

The Professor did not answer, and Abernathy continued.

"But no matter. I see that you are over your little rebellion. Or at least, you will be if you know what is good for you. There is work to do. I must inspect the troops. I need you to check over all the secondary power controls." Abernathy nodded to the other side of the walkway, to the opposite exit. "You remember where they are, I suppose? Take Miss Brunel with you. You will be quite safe, my dear Professor, I am sure. She is an intelligent child. I do believe she knows how best to survive in the world. And here that means not rocking the boat."

Abernathy laughed at his own joke, so heartily that he doubled over the railing, his high whinny echoing among his preparations for war.

Chapter 18

TIME AND TIDE

The Professor took Rémy along the wooden platform and away from Abernathy's army. Yet more guards were stationed here — they seemed to be outside each door and at every tunnel entrance. They stood, impassive, watching Rémy's progress with the Professor carefully, but with no real interest. Rémy's companion led her along another tunnel until he reached a wooden door flanked by red-robed guards. The Professor unlocked the door and entered, leaving it open as an indication that she should follow. Rémy and the Professor had not spoken a word to each other since leaving Abernathy. Rémy stepped inside, shutting the door behind her.

Inside was a workshop, though this one was less cluttered than the Professor's own at Limehouse, and looked less used. There were benches laid out with tools, and metal cabinets against the walls containing strange gauges and dials of a sort Rémy had never seen before. The Professor went to one and had to wipe the dust from its glass face before he could read it properly. He muttered something to himself and went to one of the workbenches.

"I have not been here in some time," he said, quietly enough that the guards outside would not hear, "if you're wondering about the dust. I intended never to come back. But here I am, trapped again."

"It was you, wasn't it?" Rémy asked, as the Professor began to work. "You built all these machines for him. You made his plan work."

The Professor paused and then slowly turned to face her. "Yes," he said. "Yes, I certainly made a considerable contribution."

"But why? Why would you do such a thing?"

The Professor shook his head, as if searching for the right words. "I thought it was all just talk," he said. "When I met him — where I met him — there was nothing to do but talk. So that's what we did."

"I don't understand," Rémy said with a frown.

The Professor sighed. "I did not lie when I said I was a military man," he said. "I was. But only because my father forced me to enlist. I wanted to be a scholar." He laughed sadly. "A professor, in fact. I was good at the sciences — geology, physics — those things. I didn't want to carry a gun."

"What happened?" Rémy asked.

The Professor shrugged. "What you might expect," he said, keeping his voice low. "I had what the army called 'discipline issues.' I ended up in a miserable jail in India, and that's where I met Abernathy."

Rémy nodded. She felt she should be more surprised, but somehow things were finally beginning to make sense. "This is where you talked?"

"Yes. He was always complaining about how the Empire was run. He kept talking about Alexander the Great and Genghis Khan — how the British Empire would fail and fall in on itself if it didn't keep expanding in the right direction. And to do that it needed machines. Amazing, fantastical machines of war that no foreign army could withstand. And, God help me, I told him how it could be done."

Rémy frowned. "But that was in a distant land — in prison! How did that turn into . . ." she waved her hand at their surroundings, "this?"

"Abernathy was released before me. Family connections, you see. There are plenty of disgraced sons of lords out there. He had money. I thought that was the last I'd see of him. But then he bought me out. It must have cost a fortune. And so . . ."

"You were in his debt."

The Professor nodded. "He told me at first that there were ministers in Parliament willing to back his proposals," he told her, his voice still barely above a whisper. "I'm sure there were, in fact, at that time. Talk is cheap, after all. And it was exciting for me. I became a new person. I stopped using my name — my father had, in any case, disowned me. And I came to London and began to work on the things I had always wanted to work on."

"But then something went wrong," said Rémy. "Didn't it?"

"Yes. It happened overnight, just when I had reached a breakthrough on one of the blueprints. He had a meeting in Whitehall, and he took the plans with him. He was ecstatic. He thought they were going to hail us — well, him, at least — a hero. But he came back enraged, though he refused to tell me what had happened. I think they laughed at his proposals, and he was so angry it sent him mad. That was when I should have left. I should have burned everything, all the plans, all my prototype models. But he persuaded me to go with him to a site he'd found. It was under the East End. He'd heard that a worker had found a trace of strange silver in the earth below the lime works."

"Titanium."

"Yes. Abernathy started buying every patch of land around here that he could. Then he realized that there were enough tunnels below London that he could move into them immediately. So, he did. Then he started mining."

"And you still helped him?"

"I had no choice. He knew I could process the element into metal form. And I knew too much. He could not let me just walk away."

"You could have told the police. You could have told Thaddeus, at least. He would have done something, you know he would. Why didn't you?"

The Professor looked shame-faced. "I had too much to lose, Rémy. Too much. I tried to, in my own way. When you came along — when I heard he had stolen the diamond — I thought perhaps that there was a light in the darkness, some hope. But that was not to be."

Rémy stepped away from him, leaning back on her heel as she tried to think it all through.

"What I don't understand," she whispered, "is how no one knows. There must be people who are aware that he was in jail in India, and that he is not as old as he seems, surely? What about his father? He must know that his son's face is a lie!"

The Professor shook his head. "There were two Lord Abernathys, Rémy. Most believed it was the younger who died. Only a handful know the truth."

With a jolt of shock, Rémy realized what he meant. "You mean . . . the younger took his father's place?"

"Quite," said the Professor. "All it took was a little make-up," the Professor grimaced briefly. "I am not proud of what I have helped to build, Rémy. But I could see no way out. I still cannot. I briefly thought that Desai could —" he trailed off, shaking his head.

"And what about Thaddeus?" she asked. "He trusted you. He . . . he cared about you."

The Professor smiled. "Such a smart boy, and such a good young man. He is easy to love, is he not? I thought . . . if I could help one person, if I could do one good thing."

Rémy shook her head. "It is not enough."

The Professor turned away. "It is all I can do. It's too late for anything else."

Rémy tugged at his arm, forcing him to face her

again. "It is not too late!" she said in a harsh whisper, glancing toward the door. "Tell me what I can do! Tell me how I can stop Abernathy!"

"I cannot," the Professor told her softly. "If I do he will know it was me!"

Rémy shook her head. "I know you can be a good man, Professor. I have seen it in you. Do not be a coward now. Tell me! He needed the diamond, yes? He needed the Ocean of Light. Desai said it was powerful. Is it the key? Is it?"

The Professor shook himself free of her grip, stepping away from her. "Rémy . . ."

"Just tell me where it is," she begged. "You do not have to do anything else. Just tell me where the diamond is. If I take it, he won't be able to use his machines, will he?"

The Professor sagged against the workbench behind him. "You'd never be able to get to it, even if I told you."

"I have to try! We have to try," she begged. "Can't you see that? Abernathy is really going to do this, Professor. This is no longer just talk, no longer just a game, you must see?"

Still the Professor shook his head, turning to check on another dial. Rémy moved to stand in front of him.

"Look at me," she said. "How can you betray your country like this? Your friends? Do you think no one will die when Abernathy attacks? Do you think he will let people choose who they serve?"

He shook his head. "Don't you think I know this?" he asked, his voice still lowered but full of flame. "I have tried — I tried to walk away, and I have tried to get help. But it did not work, and I am just one man! There is nothing I can do."

"There is only nothing if you do not try," Rémy told him desperately. "Help me! And if you won't, then at least tell me where the diamond is."

The Professor hesitated a moment more, looking directly into Rémy's eyes. Then he nodded, turned, and pulled a large leather-bound notebook from a pile, flipping it open to reveal pages and pages of pencil scribbles and sketches on yellowed paper. He stopped at what looked like a rough map and beckoned her to look. She recognized the river snaking its way around the Isle of Dogs and the mine hidden beneath the crammed slums of Whitechapel. The map of Abernathy's underground empire was as twisted as his mind.

"Here," the Professor said, pointing at a filigree of smaller tunnels, separated from the rest of the complex by a long, narrow corridor. "These are Abernathy's private chambers. This is where he had me build the power connections to the submarines — the underwater boats. His rooms are directly above the launch bays. He wanted to ensure that no one had access to the power source but himself."

Rémy turned back to the map. "What's that?" she asked, pointing to a thick line that the Professor had drawn, snaking through the deepest part of Abernathy's subterranean world, even below the cells where Thaddeus was now trapped. It meandered like the other tunnels, but seemed to lead straight into the Thames.

"That's the Black Ditch," the Professor told her. "It's one of London's many ancient, underground rivers. Over the centuries it has sunk, but it is still there. It is why Abernathy chose that exact place to build the submarines."

Rémy frowned, not understanding. "What do you mean?"

The Professor's answering words were drowned out by Abernathy himself. His voice blasted out above them. Rémy turned to see a cone of metal fastened to the wall from which Abernathy's speech blared loudly.

"Professor," he bellowed, his voice tinny in the air. "Give me a pressure reading, if you please. And then one from the power gauge."

The Professor jumped, backing away from Rémy. He turned and went to one of the metal cabinets, checking some of the dials before he moved to a small black box in the wall that was fastened at head height and had a metal cone just like the one Abernathy's voice had poured from, though smaller. The box was directly below the larger cone, and Rémy could see some kind of tube running between the two. The Professor cranked the stiff handle on the box, pulling it toward him with effort, and spoke into the cone.

"Pressure holding at five hundred, Lord Abernathy," he said loudly. "And power is at one hundred percent. The Darya-ye Noor is working just as we hoped."

"Marvelous!" Abernathy bellowed, his voice echoing around the control room. "Excellent news, Professor, and it leads me to conclude that we have no more need to delay at all."

Rémy saw the Professor frown. "My Lord?" he said into the cone. "What do you —"

"All men take note! Phase One commencing," the villain announced. "Take your stations! I say again, Phase One commencing. Every man required to take his station! Professor, join me, if you please. Oh, and do bring Miss Brunel. She would not enjoy being left behind."

The Professor cranked the handle back away from him and spun toward her. Rémy saw that all the color had drained from his face. "What is it?" she cried. "What's happening?"

"I did not think — no, it must be a drill, surely," the Professor stuttered. "He can't . . . he can't be starting now! It is too early! We are not ready! Nothing is —"

He pushed past Rémy and went to another metal cabinet on the wall that was covered in gauges and dials. He squinted at one, shaking his head. Then he tapped it — once, twice. Rémy stepped up behind him, seeing the hand on the gauge wobbling quickly toward the red.

"What is it, Professor?" she asked. "What is going on? What is Abernathy doing?"

The Professor wiped at his sweating brow. "He's launching. I cannot believe it! It's too early. We're not ready, we're not —"

Rémy gripped the Professor's arm. "Launching? What do you mean by launching?"

The Professor looked down at her. "The plan. Abernathy's attack on London. He's launching Phase

One of the plan. And that means we have to go. Now." He ran back to the desk and began to gather up as many papers as he could carry. Rémy followed him.

"But what does that mean, Professor?"

The Professor slammed down his pile of papers and indicated the map, pointing straight at the dark, thick line of the Black Ditch.

"To launch the submarines, he needs water. That's why he built them as close to where the river passes the tunnel as possible. He's going to cause an explosion in the wall holding the river back. He's going to blow a hole right through it. He's going to let the water come to him."

Rémy stared at the map again. "But the river is far below the launch tunnels. Isn't it?"

"Yes. There wasn't anywhere closer that he could build the boats. None of the other caverns were big enough. But he is banking on the pressure of the water being so great as to force a chasm large enough that the tunnels between here and there will collapse when the water rushes in."

Rémy stared, suddenly afraid. "He's going to flood the tunnels?"

The Professor nodded. "It's the only way for him to launch the submarines."

"But — but what about everyone down here?" Rémy asked, a fearful tremor in her heart. "What about Thaddeus? He's still in that cell. And what about everyone in the mines? What about J, Professor?"

The Professor shook his head. "They were supposed to be evacuated. I believed that they would . . . there's nothing I can do now."

"There — there must be!" she shouted, no longer caring if the guards outside heard her. "You built all of this! You must be able to stop it!"

"Even if I could, it would do no good!" the Professor shouted back. "The sequence has started! Once the flooding starts, there's no stopping it. All of the lower levels will flood first. We have to go, Rémy. We have to save ourselves. It's all we can do now! I'm so sorry."

Rémy pulled herself out of his grasp, shaking her head. From beneath them came a rumble like thunder, but deep below the earth. The ground began to shake.

"I have to help them," she shouted. "Thaddeus, J, all those people. I have to get them out!"

The Professor shook his head again. "You won't make it, Rémy," he told her. "You'll never rescue them all before the tunnels flood!"

Chapter 19

COME HELL OR HIGH WATER

*R*émy stared at the Professor as the rumbling around them continued. She could feel her eyes filling with tears.

"I can't save them," she said. "I can't . . . I can't save them."

The Professor shook his head, sadness darkening his eyes. "I know. I'm sorry. Believe me, I am."

Rémy drew in a breath and for a moment, Thaddeus's face loomed large in her mind, frozen like a picture from the last time she had seen him. His eyes had been full of pain, and her heart almost broke in two at the memory. She'd done that to him. She'd hurt him deliberately because she couldn't bear the hugeness of what else she was feeling, couldn't cope with the idea that part of her might already be tied to him forever, without her even realizing it had happened. And then she'd left him there, when all he'd ever wanted was to help people. To help her. To save her. She'd left him there. And now he would die alone.

She shook her head as the tears ran down her cheeks. "Thaddeus . . . Thaddeus would try to stop him. Abernathy. Wouldn't he? No matter what. No matter . . . what he had to leave behind."

The Professor nodded sadly. "Of course he would. What a good, good man."

Rémy swiped a hand across her face, angrily flicking away the tears. "Give me the map. I have to get to the diamond. I have to stop this."

The Professor shook his head, "Rémy, it's too late."

"Just give it to me!" she snapped, her heart exploding in an inferno of fury. She lunged toward the table and ripped the yellowed pages of the map from his notebook. "If you will not help me, so be it. But I can't — I can't just do nothing."

There was a noise behind them as the door opened, and the two red-robed guards strode in. They looked as forbidding as ever, but Rémy could see fear in their eyes.

"Did you not hear Lord Abernathy's command, Professor?" one rumbled, his voice deep with a foreign accent. "We must go. The tunnels are already flooding. The first level has gone and in five minutes the submarines will be sealed for launch."

The Professor turned to gather up his papers again, catching Rémy's eye. "Of — of course," he said. "I am just . . . trying to save some of my plans. They are for Phase Two, you see. Help me, please."

Rémy backed away as the two men moved forward. One of the men glanced toward her, frowning at what she held in her hand.

"What do you have there?" he asked.

"Nothing," she said, putting the papers behind her back.

"Let me see . . ." He loomed closer, twice as tall as Rémy and at least three times heavier. She darted past him, heading for the door, but he was on her at once. She felt his heavy hand on her shoulder, spinning her around to face him.

His face was as hard as iron — but then a heavy clunk, something solid hitting something immovable. The guard's face blanked suddenly, his features sagging all at once. He dropped his hand as his eyes closed and the next moment he was on his knees.

Rémy looked at the Professor. His arms were raised. Then she saw the heavy book that had smashed into the guard's head lying beside the fallen man, tainted with his blood.

The second guard yelled a short word of rage and lunged for the Professor.

"Go!" the Professor cried, as the huge man's hands closed around his throat. "Go now!"

Rémy hesitated a second more, watching as the Professor sank beneath the weight of his opponent. He was struggling, but weakly, no match for the massive guard.

"Go," he croaked again, his voice fading. "Rémy — just go!"

She turned her back and fled through the door, the map held tightly in her hand. Outside, the sound of rumbling was louder. The ground was shifting, moving slightly under her feet.

★ ★ ★

They tried everything, but it was no good. Abernathy's cell was sealed tight. The bars seemed to have no end, plunging too deep into the compacted earth for them to dig their way out, and the titanium was relentlessly strong.

Thaddeus stepped away from his latest attempt to force them apart and threw his hands into the air in frustration.

"This is useless! We're never going to get out of here!"

He turned away from Desai and rubbed his face with his hands. God only knew what Abernathy and his men were up to right at this moment.

"There is something I have not tried," Desai said quietly, after a moment. "Though I am not sure —"

Thaddeus spun on his heel. "Whatever it is, Desai, it's our last option! Tell me!"

Desai shook his head. His skin was still pale from his recent ordeal, and their efforts at jail breaking had weakened him further. "It is something I have not attempted for a long, long time, Thaddeus. I am warning you now that it may come to nothing."

Thaddeus nodded. "It is all the hope we have, Desai. What can I do?"

The Indian man glanced toward the cell door at the lock that secured their prison. "This is down to me alone. Stand back, please."

He went to the lock, bending over it as Thaddeus backed himself against the far wall. For a long time it seemed as if Desai were doing nothing at all. He gripped the bars of the door and bent his head. To Thaddeus it looked as if he were merely praying or else meditating in a peculiar pose. Thaddeus was beginning to wonder if he should speak into the silence, when something began to happen.

At first, he wasn't even sure what he was seeing. Desai tensed, his dark knuckles fading white where he gripped the silver bars, his shoulders hunched and rigid, his head dipped. Thaddeus could see that the man was shaking, a myriad of tremors wracking his body.

Then, without warning, a blue flame burned bright in the dull cell. Thaddeus jumped, uttering a cry, as the flame fizzed and cracked beside Desai's hand. It seemed to have come from Desai himself, but Thaddeus had not seen him strike a match. Slowly, it engulfed the lock, dancing around and through it like a veil of fire.

There was a tinny creak, the sound of metal shearing against metal — and then the lock sprang open and Desai fell back to the floor, motionless. The door swung on its hinges as the blue flame licked its way up the bars and vanished in a dense puff of smoke.

"Desai!" Thaddeus rushed to the fallen man, taking in his ashen face and shaking hands. But at least his eyes were open. "Are you all right?"

Desai nodded with evident difficulty. "Just weak-ened still more, I fear. I have not performed that trick for many, many years."

Thaddeus looked over his shoulder at the broken prison. "That was amazing. What — how did you —"

His question was cut short by a deep, low noise that shook the ground. It began with a whump, like the sound of air being let out of a long-sealed room, but much louder. Then came the first rumble, somehow both far away and very near. It sounded like thunder, but unlike thunder, it did not roll away into silence.

"What was that?" Thaddeus asked.

"I do not know," Desai said quietly. "But I do not think we should stay to find out. You must help me up."

Thaddeus helped Desai to his feet. He could feel the man trembling beneath his robes and had to put an arm beneath his shoulders so that he could walk.

"This must be the start of Abernathy's plans," Desai said as they slowly set off down the stone corridor.

"We have to go after him," Thaddeus said as the thunder below them continued. "Whatever Abernathy's up to, we have to stop it."

Desai improved as they went on, gradually moving faster. Thaddeus kept thinking about the sight of Rémy's retreating back, following in Abernathy's footsteps. He had to find her. He had to tell her that he wasn't afraid — not of the curse she carried, not of her past life, or indeed whatever life she chose. He just wanted her to be safe. He just wanted her to be happy. He just wanted . . . her.

Thaddeus's thoughts were interrupted by the sound of running footsteps. He thought at first that somehow their escape had been discovered. but instead the group of Abernathy's thugs that came thundering toward them seemed intent on another purpose. The first man neared and Thaddeus realized that what showed on his face was not fury, but fear. He wasn't looking at Thaddeus, either, but past him.

"Out of the way," this man growled as Thaddeus stood in his path. "For God's sake, man, let me through!"

Thaddeus barely had time to move before the thug was past him and away down the corridor without even a pause. The others were the same — huge men with terror on their faces and nothing in their minds but to flee. But from what?

"What's happening?" Thaddeus shouted as the men continued to stream past him. "What are you running from?"

None of them answered. Thaddeus reached out,

trying to catch one by the arm, but his hand was shaken off and the man he had tried to stop did not even look back at him.

"These are the men from the mine," Desai told him, raising his voice over the sound of heavy running feet and the rumble all around them. "Abernathy's slave masters."

Thaddeus looked around. The last man was large and fat, too heavy to run fast. The policeman recognized him.

"Jonesy!"

The man glanced in his direction as he puffed after his friends, but he made no signs of stopping. "Get out of my way, boy."

Thaddeus stood in front of him. "What's going on? Where are you going? What's happening, Jonesy?"

Jonesy might have been pudgy and red in the face, but he was still strong enough to push Thaddeus out of the way. Thaddeus stumbled but kept his balance. He lunged after the fleeing man, catching him by his dirty shirt. The momentum was enough to spin Jonesy around and slam him against the wall with a jaw-juddering crash as his head hit the hard rock. Jonesy dropped to his knees with an angry roar, grabbing Thaddeus around the stomach and pulling him down.

They scuffled in the dirt, and although Jonesy was heavier, Thaddeus was quicker. He scrambled around until he had the man on his knees, his neck crushed into the bend of his arm.

"Just tell me," Thaddeus said, out of breath, "what is going on. Tell me, and I'll let you go."

"It's Abernathy, you fool," Jonesy puffed. "He's only gone and blown the river wall. This place is flooding, and fast! We've all got to get out. We've got to get out now! The lower level has already gone. This one's next."

Thaddeus frowned. "You mean the Thames?"

"Of course not, you half-wit. The Black Ditch. It's pouring in here, right now. The mine will go, I'm telling you. We've got to get out. Let me go, will ya? I've got to get out, man!"

Thaddeus gritted his teeth and squeezed the pleading man's neck harder. "What about the miners? The slaves? I don't see them running. Where are they?"

"Oh, come on — you must be joking!" Jonesy managed, around Thaddeus's choke hold. "There wasn't time to unlock 'em!"

Thaddeus let Jonesy go, spinning him around again.

"You left them there? You just — left them there?"

Jonesy shrugged, reaching up to rub his fat fingers against his sore neck. "None of 'em have got much life left in 'em, anyway."

Thaddeus managed to reign in his anger, but only just. "Where's Abernathy?" he asked.

"Tucked up nice and cozy in one of them fancy subs of his," Jonesy spat. "He don't care about the likes of us."

"Where?" Thaddeus rasped again. "Tell us where."

Jonesy nodded down the corridor in the direction that he'd just come from. "You go that way and just keep going up. There'll be no way out, though, not once the water comes. You're best following me."

Thaddeus stood, hauling Jonesy to his feet. "I wouldn't follow you if you were the last man on Earth. I'll take these, you filthy coward," he spat, ripping the keys from Jonesy's belt.

"Coward I may be. But dying I ain't." Jonesy shouted as he began to run again, his bulk receding along the darkened tunnel.

"Go for Abernathy," Thaddeus said to Desai. "I've got to try and free the slaves."

Desai shook his head, his dark eyes troubled. "If what he says is true — if the lower level is gone already, there is no time left. Even if you reach the mine."

Thaddeus looked up at him. "I know. But I have to try. I at least have to try."

Desai paused again for a moment and then nodded, resting a hand on Thaddeus's shoulder. "You are a brave man, Thaddeus Rec. I wish I could have had longer to know you."

Thaddeus smiled thinly. "And I you, Desai."

★ ★ ★

Around her, distant shouts echoed against the walls, but they seemed to be fading. With every minute the rumbling grew. The ground was shaking more than ever. Rémy stumbled, the loose pebbles beneath her feet beginning to jump as if they were alive. Time was running out.

The map was rough, but it showed Rémy that the only way to Abernathy's chambers was through the launch bays themselves — the room where Abernathy had shown her the submarines. The door she had seen on the opposite side of the wooden walkway must have led to his private quarters. The passageway leading to the room had fallen dark. The guards had vanished. She ran to the wooden door, wrenching it open a crack and peering into the cavern beyond.

The vast room was lit, not by gaslight but by an

eerie, supernatural glow. It rose from the four underwater vessels, shining blue in the otherwise dark
space, and the noise they made was unlike any Rémy
had ever heard before. It was loud and yet somehow
empty, a booming echo that filled her head and even
drowned out the incessant rumble of approaching
water. Inside each vessel, she could see men, all hard
at work, evidently preparing for action, and on the
floor of the cavern, the suits were no longer still and
silent. Every one had a man inside and each carried
two weapons, a dangerous-looking curved scimitar
and one of the Professor's gas rifles. Abernathy's
army was complete.

Abernathy himself was nowhere to be seen, but
then Rémy didn't pause to look too hard. She ran for
the opening on the other side of the room, hoping to
reach it before anyone even saw her in the gloom. The
platform was deserted, all the men apparently occupied below.

A movement caught her eye, and she glanced down
between the planks of the walkway to see one of
Abernathy's red-robed men not yet inside his metal
suit, shouting and gesturing at her frantically. None of
the other men seemed to be taking any notice, though.
They were all too intent on their tasks, on making sure

they were prepared for the flood. The lone guard ran up the steps that led from the walkway to the cavern floor, heading straight for Rémy.

She dodged him once, trying to use her momentum to push him as she passed, hoping to tip him off balance. But it didn't work; he was too strong. He caught her around the waist and she struggled, kicking out at his legs with her booted feet and trying to claw her way out of his savage embrace. He took no notice, carrying her to the steps.

"Let me go," she screamed, her voice lost to the eerie noise of the submarines. "Let — me — go!"

The guard paused at the top of the stairs and Rémy struggled harder, hoping to tip them both over the edge. At least that way she might have a chance of breaking free as they tumbled.

"Idiot," she cried. "You stupid, stupid . . ."

She felt, rather than heard, striding footsteps vibrating through the wooden planks behind them. The next minute, Rémy found her captor's grip loosening just a fraction as he turned toward the footsteps. She kicked out hard, catching his shin. He flinched and fell, crashing so heavily down the wooden steps that they splintered beneath his weight.

Rémy caught the handrail and hauled herself up

to the walkway. What she found there she could not believe.

"Desai? But . . . but . . ."

"No time," he mouthed over the noise.

Rémy followed his gaze and realized what he meant. The guard's heavy fall had drawn the attention of Abernathy's foot soldiers. They were crowding around his crumpled form, looking up into the darkness of the walkway to see what had happened. She backed into the deeper shadows against the cavern's walls, Desai by her side.

"Go," said Desai.

Rémy and Desai reached the far wooden door and crashed through it, out of the cavern and into another room entirely.

★ ★ ★

Thaddeus reached the mine. There was no sign of water. He ran down the steps, the desperate cries of the chained slaves echoing toward him.

"Help us! Please! Please, let us go!"

"There's a flood coming! I heard them say so! Please, mister — show a little mercy!"

"Save us! Please!"

There were so many pleading faces that Thaddeus

could not see them all clearly. He ran to the nearest man and saw that the metal bracelet around his chaffed ankle held a steel ring through which ran the chain that trapped him and about fifty others.

"Where's the lock?" Thaddeus shouted at the man frantically. "Where is it?"

"Archie — he's at the front today," said the man. "Archie, c'mere!"

Another scrawny man stumbled forward, dragging the chain with him. Thaddeus knelt in front of him, fitting key after key into the lock. It took him six attempts to find the right one. The lock turned stiffly and then sprang open. The man staggered free, still with the cuff around his ankle but free of the chain.

"God bless you, sir," he said, running for the exit as the slaves began to pull the rest of the chain free.

"Wait," Thaddeus called before Archie could reach the doorway. "Wait — how many chains are there?"

Archie glanced around, "Can't be more'n twenty."

"I'll never unlock them all on my own. Stay — help me. Please."

For a second Thaddeus thought Archie was going to ignore him and run, but then he nodded. "Give me some of them keys," he said.

Thaddeus thrust half the bunch of jangling metal toward him and then ran to another of the slave lines. He looked around but couldn't see J anywhere. There were so many people to save.

He and Archie were down to the last two chains when the rumbling turned into a cruel, cracking sound like an earthquake. Then followed a loud, forbidding splash of water. The weight of the flood juddered the rock face, sending chunks of jagged stone thudding to the ground amid the terrified slaves. The younger were helping the older, the able-bodied aiding the injured, but none were moving fast enough. *Any minute now,* Thaddeus thought. *Any minute now and we are all lost.*

Thaddeus undid the last chain and then spun around, still searching for J. *Maybe Archie has already let him out,* he told himself. *Maybe J's already on the run.*

And then a movement caught his eye, in the far corner of the mine. It was J, but he wasn't running. He was trying to help another boy, one who looked to be about his age. J had his arm around him and was trying to drag him up because the boy obviously could not walk alone.

"J!" Thaddeus shouted, running toward them. "J —"

There was a huge splitting noise as if heaven itself

had broken in two. Thaddeus looked up to see a crack running floor to ceiling, up the mine's wall right behind the two children.

And then the water came.

DON'T LOOK DOWN

"*W*here is Thaddeus?" Rémy asked as soon as they were inside Abernathy's rooms. "If you survived, he must have, too. Where is he, Desai?"

Desai's eyes were weighted with sadness. "I am sorry, Rémy. He went to the mine. He could not leave those people to drown without at least trying to rescue them."

Rémy swallowed hard. "Then . . . then . . . He was alive, but . . ."

Desai nodded gently. "I am sorry. He was . . . is a brave, brave man. But I fear that the flood . . ."

Rémy turned away abruptly. "Don't," she said, her voice cracking. "Don't say it. I don't want to hear . . ."

"Very well," Desai said softly. "Then let us concentrate on the task at hand."

Abernathy's private chambers were surreal — a vast living room that would not have been out of place in any of the most expensive houses in Paris, apart from the fact that it was circular and had no windows. The walls were lined with bookcases specially constructed to fit the space. There was a curved desk, comfortable chairs, and heavy velvet curtains that hid an alcove containing a large, opulently dressed bed. Gas lamps hung from the walls, lending a dim, flickering light.

There was, however, no sign of the Darya-ye Noor, nor anything that looked as if it could serve as a power link.

"Where is it?" Rémy asked, turning around in a circle. "It should be here! The Professor said it would be here!"

Desai shook his head. "It must be concealed somewhere."

Rémy took out the map, running to the desk and smoothing out the now-crumpled pages. She pointed to the sketches showing Abernathy's chambers. "It says there's a corridor. There can't be! This is all there is. Argh!" Rémy shouted in frustration, "He's done it again! The Professor has tricked us — again!"

Desai rested a hand on her shoulder. "Perhaps not. Perhaps this map is not quite accurate. We must search."

"There's no time!"

"Time is all we have left, Rémy. Let us not waste it!"

She nodded, attempting to calm herself. *"D'accord. D'accord.* But where? There is nothing here but books!"

Desai turned and went to one of the bookcases. "Perhaps that is what Abernathy wants you to think. Perhaps we should see what is behind them. Yes?"

He prized his fingers between the wall and wood. Rémy crossed the room to help him. They pulled the bookcase from the wall, but found nothing behind it.

"The next one," Desai said. "Hurry!"

The next bookcase yielded nothing, nor did the next. The noise of the rumbling had grown so loud and so close that it drowned even the sound of Abernathy's machines.

"It's too late," Rémy said in despair. "We're in the wrong place. We must be!"

Desai didn't answer. Instead, he went to the next bookcase in the row and pulled. He paused for a second and then looked at her.

"Quickly," he said, "help me!"

They didn't bother to keep the bookcase

standing. There was no time. Instead, between them they wrenched it forward until it toppled to the floor with a deafening crash, books tumbling to the floor as they slipped from the shelves.

"*Mon Dieu!*" Rémy exclaimed.

Behind it, set in the wall, was a chamber. It was circular with a glass front and silver walls that closed it off from the surrounding rock. The chamber also had a circular silver floor, a platform that fitted snugly within the space. The platform had its own half-walls, which rose a few feet, culminating in a smooth hand-rail. It looked to Rémy like a smaller version of the machines that dockers use to load ships in port.

Rémy pressed her face against the glass, trying to see inside. "The diamond — where is it?"

Desai stepped to her side. "I do not think this is what we are looking for, Rémy."

"What? But it must be! Why else would Abernathy have a secret chamber hidden behind a bookcase?"

Desai didn't answer for a second. Instead, he tilted his head so that he could see up inside the chamber. "Look, there," he said. "It has no roof. I think this is a method of escape." He indicated the silver platform, and then a box with a lever that was fastened to the handrail. "One stands on the floor, and it moves. Upward."

Rémy's mind whirred. "It leads to the surface? It is a way out?"

Desai frowned. "Either that, or it leads to the power chamber," he said. "Although I find it unlikely he would want to manhandle a bookcase out of the way every time he needed to check on the machine's workings."

He turned to look at the final bookcase they had not tried. Without a word they both went to it. Rémy was expecting that they would have to tip it as they had the other, with considerable effort. But to her surprise, when Desai pushed, it swung forward smoothly.

"It's on a hinge!"

"Indeed," said Desai, "and there is the reason why."

He was right. Behind the bookcase was a wooden door. Rémy opened it, feeling a cold gush of wind rush past her and into the room.

Beyond, it was dark. Desai pulled one of the dimming lamps from the wall and held it out as they moved forward. It was another passageway, damp and dark. Rémy took a few steps and then froze.

"Oh, no," she whispered.

Before them at some distance was another door, made of plain and simple wood and with no sign of a keyhole. But between them and the door was a great chasm in the ground. There had obviously once been a narrow bridge over the abyss, but it had been hacked apart.

"So," said Desai gravely. "Abernathy once again proves himself to be insane, but not a fool."

Rémy walked to the edge of the chasm and looked down. It seemed endless. A deep, heavy draught rolled up and over its edge as she stared into it. God only knew how deep it was or what was at the bottom. She looked to the other side. There was no way to jump it. She stepped onto the wooden stairs that had once led to the now broken bridge, and looked to the other side. The steps over there were still intact, hanging, splintered, into the chasm. If only she could reach them.

"I need a rope," she said. "Or a wire. Something, anything that I can throw across and pull taut."

She ran back into Abernathy's chamber and began to search, ripping drawers from their chests, turning their contents onto the floor. Desai followed her, joining in with more vigor than a dead man should ever have.

"Here!" he said. "Look — here!"

Rémy looked up to see him holding a rope, still coiled in on itself. It was wide and rough, more so than she would usually walk, but right now she would take anything.

She ran back to the chasm, uncoiling the rope as she went. Then Rémy pulled off her boots, tying the end of the rope to one of them. She gauged its length as she unraveled it — it would reach, but only just. Then she leapt back onto the top step and dangled the rope, boot attached, from her hand. She could feel Desai behind her, tense but wisely staying silent.

Rémy felt everything fade away — the endless rumbling, the quaking of the ground, the darkness of the chasm below her. She could do this. She'd done this since she was a child. This is what she was good at.

She swung the rope and let go. Her boot sailed through the air, its weight taking the rope as she let it feed out between her hands. It struck the last piece of wooden rail left on the other side of the abyss, winding itself tight.

"Yes!" Rémy whispered, pulling the rope as hard as she could to see if it would budge. It stayed put. Then she began to tie off her end, knotting it firmly around the wooden stump of the stairs. It wasn't perfect but it was tight, and that was all that mattered right now.

"Are you sure you want to do this?" Desai asked as

she stepped up to the rope. "I will not be able to follow you."

She looked at him and smiled. Behind them, the sounds of Abernathy's machines began to change, warring with the roaring flood. There was a clanking, whirring noise, as if a thousand metal birds had taken off at once.

"I am our last chance," she said. "Use the escape hatch. If I don't succeed, warn whoever you can. The police, the government. Anyone. Yes?"

Desai gripped her hand for a second and then nodded. She turned away, stepping swiftly out over the void. The rope did not sag, and her bare feet gripped the coarse fibers well. She walked forward — one foot, two feet, the abyss yawning wide below her.

There was a sudden commotion behind her. She heard footsteps and then a shout of shock from Desai and thought that Abernathy had sent his men for them after all. She turned gracefully, her arms held out, spinning on the narrow rope without ever losing her footing.

But it wasn't Abernathy or his men. It was Thaddeus Rec.

It was Thaddeus, carrying one small, bedraggled boy while another — J, she realized, it was J, alive! —

wearily gripped his trouser leg. All three were drenched, muddy water streaked their faces, their hair, their clothes. Thaddeus looked exhausted, pale-faced, and gaunt, and he had frozen stock-still in the light cast from Abernathy's chamber, staring straight at her.

Rémy's heart stopped. She thought she was going to black out. She felt her knees buckle, her feet losing their fragile grip on the rope.

"No!" The shout was from Thaddeus. He rushed forward, thrusting the boy he held into Desai's arms and lunging toward the chasm's edge as Rémy's feet lost their grip. She twisted herself into a half-turn, until she was parallel with the rope, and forced her feet to follow it. Her legs split along the rope as she threw her arms out for balance. The rope shivered but held.

Rémy breathed hard, sucking in great lungfuls of cold, cloying air as she forced herself to regain her calm. She couldn't look at Thaddeus. She was shaking too hard, afraid of losing her balance again.

"Are you trying to kill me?" she asked, though it wasn't at all what she had meant to say. "Idiot!"

"What are you doing?" he asked. "What on earth are you doing?"

"The power chamber," she said. "I have to get to it. I can still stop Abernathy."

"No," said Thaddeus. "I don't think you can. The water is right behind us. We only just escaped. Nothing can stop him now. All we can hope is that the flood won't fill the cavern. Maybe we'll be safe here in Abernathy's chambers. Maybe we can survive."

Rémy gingerly folded her legs under her, silent as she regained her feet. She turned to face Thaddeus. "No," she told him. "But Abernathy built an escape route. You can use it." She smiled at him briefly. "I am so glad," she said quietly. "I am so very glad that you are alive, Thaddeus."

"Rémy," Thaddeus said, his voice echoing across the chasm as she turned away from him. "Rémy, don't do it. Come back. There's nothing we can do now. Please. If you don't come now, you won't make it back across before the water comes."

"I don't need to," she said, finding her way along the last few feet of rope. "All I need to do is remove the diamond, and his plan will fail. I can still stop him."

She jumped onto the broken top step and then to the hard ground beyond, finally turning to look at him. Thaddeus was staring at her.

"You'll — you'll die," he said. "You'll either drown or be trapped down here, until the air runs out, or . . . or until you starve."

Rémy looked at him calmly. "Don't worry about me, little policeman. Now, go. Use the escape shaft before it is too late."

He shook his head and climbed up onto the destroyed steps instead, standing over the taut rope. "I'm coming, too."

Rémy's heart leapt into her mouth. "Don't be a fool! You'll never make it across!"

"I will if you help me." He put one foot on the rope. "Tell me how. Show me how."

"No," she said. She felt tears pricking her eyes again. "No, I will not. I cannot — it's too difficult for a beginner."

Thaddeus looked at her, his eyes alight. "I can't let you do this alone. I won't — I can't leave you behind."

"You can," she said. "You must." She looked at Desai, standing behind Thaddeus. "Desai, make him go. Take him. Please. You have to hurry! Listen!"

The sound of water was crashing closer now, a huge, drowning weight crushing everything in its path. They couldn't see it yet, but it was an unstoppable tide, a natural monster, and any moment now it would be close enough to swallow them all. But still Thaddeus did not leave the rope. Instead, he made as if to step forward, out over the abyss.

"No," Rémy cried, fear engulfing her. "Don't! You'll fall, Thaddeus! Stop wasting my time. You'll fall!"

"Then I'll untie the rope and swing across. You can pull me up."

She shook her head. She wanted him out of here, safe. Rémy grabbed her end of the rope, where it was caught fast around the end of the crumbled steps, and began to undo it. "Step back. I will not let you follow me."

"Don't!" Thaddeus shouted. "Rémy, listen to me. Listen!" he paused, shaking his head, as if screwing up his courage. "I can't live in the world, knowing you are not in it, too. I don't want to. If you're determined to sacrifice yourself, I won't let you do it alone. I can't. Do you hear me, Rémy Brunel? Do you hear me?"

Rémy stared at him, and the expanse between them seemed immeasurable. Her sight was blurred and she was crying, but still she could not say a thing. She did not want him to die. She did not want to be the reason for it, and she did not want to die knowing that he was not living on in the world because of her. But she couldn't say any of this. She couldn't.

"I love you," he said then, simply, into the incongruous silence that had spun itself around them. "I can't help it. I don't care if you don't feel the same.

I don't care if you think I can't know after only a week. I just — love you. So don't let the last time I see you be me leaving you to die alone. Just . . . don't."

The silence was shattered by a frantic shout from J. Rémy tore her gaze away from Thaddeus and looked through the open doors of Abernathy's chamber. Beyond it, a wall of water was crashing onwards, stopped only by the cavern itself. She could see the escaped river pouring out of the wall, millions of gallons of water gushing down into the launch bay where Abernathy and his men stood, safe and secure and expectant in their fantastical machines. But soon it would be full, and the only place the water had to go was where Desai, J, and Thaddeus stood on the other side of the abyss.

Chapter 21

THE LAST TIDE

*R*émy stared at Thaddeus across the chasm. "You are an idiot!" she shouted at him. "An idiot! Do you know that?"

"Are you going to let me across?"

She hesitated for another moment. The water roared behind them, gushing closer with each second, but she couldn't seem to tear her eyes away from his. Rémy nodded reluctantly.

"All right," said Thaddeus, undoing the knotted rope. "Here's what I'm going to do —"

There was another, deeper roar from behind them. Rémy looked over Thaddeus's head, through the two open doors in Abernathy's chamber and out the other side to the cavern beyond. In the gap she could see the eerie blue light of the submarines as they began to move, buoyed up by the water.

"Desai," she shouted, over the din. "Go. Go!"

Desai didn't need telling twice. He grabbed J by the hand, still holding the other boy in his free arm. J fought him, desperate to stay with Thaddeus, but Desai dragged him away, out of sight, into Abernathy's escape chamber.

"Your last chance, Thaddeus," Rémy said. "You can still go with them."

Thaddeus ignored her, tying the rope around his waist. He sat down on the edge of the broken steps, his feet dangling over the abyss. Rémy saw him take a deep breath as her own heart hammered in her chest. If the rope was to break, he would surely plunge to a stony death. For a moment Rémy thought he'd changed his mind. But then he looked up at her and, with a warm smile, let himself drop.

Rémy clenched her fists as he plummeted, praying for the rope to hold as it jerked to the end of its reach with his weight. The rope was fine, but the destroyed wooden steps creaked dangerously and for a second, as Thaddeus slammed hard against the near wall of the chasm, she thought it was going to give. She leapt forward, throwing herself flat against the edge of the chasm and grabbing the rope with both hands.

"Climb!" she shouted as she dragged on the rope, trying to hold his weight. "Thaddeus, for God's sake, climb! I can't . . . I can't hold you."

She felt the rope moving but couldn't see him. Winding it around her hands, Rémy rolled backward, pulling with all her might. The rope rasped against the chasm's jagged edge, threatening to snap at any minute. Rémy felt her arms being pulled from their sockets, every muscle straining against Thaddeus's weight.

And then, there he was. One hand appeared, and then another, as Thaddeus clawed his way over the top of the chasm to safety. Rémy didn't let go of the rope, still pulling with all her might until he was on level ground. They both collapsed, sprawling in the dirt, weak with exhaustion.

Rémy was the first to recover, getting to her knees, still breathing hard. "Are you all right?"

Thaddeus tried to move. "Yes . . . yes, I think so . . ."

She grabbed his hand, getting to her feet as she tried to haul him up. "Then hurry!"

"Wait," he said, trying to pull her closer, "Rémy — wait —"

"There's no time!" she cried. "Look!"

She pointed across the chasm and through Abernathy's chamber. Beyond, the water had become a rippling, surging wall.

They ran to the door, hands still entwined. Thaddeus fell against it, his shoulder smashing into the wood like a battering ram. The door flew open.

Inside was a room far smaller than Rémy had expected. It was circular like Abernathy's chamber, but hardly even half the size. The walls were bare earth and rock, and most of the space in the room was taken up by a spherical structure.

It looked like a cage, but more ornate — curved filigree arms of metal spindling together like fist-sized bubbles intersecting over a tanner's bucket. These bubbles became smaller and more entangled as they reached toward the room's floor and ceiling, until the pattern was so dense that nothing could pass into the spaces between, not even the glass that married each metal arm together.

The sphere narrowed into tubes, which disappeared into passageways in the floor and rounded roof. Blue sparks akin to the light inside Abernathy's submarines flowed along each spun metal arm, pulsing like the beat of a straining heart. And in the center of the sphere, on a mechanical plinth, was the Darya-ye Noor, its surfaces shimmering in the bright light.

Except that it wasn't alone.

"Is that — is that another diamond?"

Rémy nodded silently at Thaddeus's question. There, beside the unmistakably pink beauty of the Ocean of Light was another diamond, equally as stunning.

* * *

"There must be a way to break the glass," Thaddeus said, looking around frantically. Rémy didn't answer, and when he looked back, she was still staring, transfixed, at the jewels within their glass cage. "Rémy!"

She jumped, looking up at him, and then around the room. "I — there's nothing in here! There's nothing to use!"

"Stand back," Thaddeus told her.

He moved to one of the largest glass panels, still only as big as his hand, and braced his elbow against it. Then taking a deep breath, Thaddeus punched his hand forward sharply before bringing his bent elbow back against the glass. The tiny window splintered, shattering as the pieces rained down inside the sphere.

Rémy was beside him in an instant as Thaddeus

tried to fit his hand through the gap, but it was no good — he cut and bloodied his knuckle but could not get his hand inside.

"Move!" said Rémy. "Let me."

A huge noise reverberated behind them. Thaddeus turned to see a cascade of water smashing through Abernathy's chamber with such force that a raging torrent flowed over the mouth of the cavern and slewed straight into the power chamber. The icy wave crashed against them, slamming them both against the sphere and almost knocking them off their feet.

Thaddeus grabbed Rémy by the arm, holding on tight as the water was sucked back out again and down into the chasm outside. He looked over his shoulder to see another wave coming at them, brown and murky and even bigger than the last. He pushed Rémy up the sphere.

"Get as high as you can!" Thaddeus shouted over the roar of water echoing around them. "There's another —"

The second wave hit them even harder than the first, but Thaddeus held on to the metal and managed to drag himself up behind Rémy's nimble form. They straddled the sphere, watching as the water was sucked back out of the room.

"I have to get the diamond," she shouted amid the maelstrom. "I have to go back down."

"You can't," Thaddeus shouted back, "the next wave will be even bigger!"

"I only need a moment," she said, already clambering toward the smashed glass.

He reached out, trying to catch her wrist, but she was too quick for him. "Don't," he shouted, beginning to follow her. "Rémy, don't —"

He saw her fingers touch the Ocean of Light as the third wave hit with even more force than those that had come before. Rémy disappeared beneath a torrent of brown silt, and Thaddeus had to hold on to stop himself being pulled from the sphere.

"Rémy," he shouted. "Rémy . . ."

The water receded and, for a moment, he thought she had been taken with it. Instead, she appeared, fingers still wrapped around the stone, coughing up the fetid water. She wrenched the diamond free of the plinth's mechanical grip and pulled it out, holding it aloft triumphantly.

A new noise echoed around them, a dying, fading noise, like the wind dropping after a violent night. The blue sparks that had flowed through the sphere sputtered and slowed and then stopped altogether.

"You've done it!" Thaddeus shouted.

"Did you ever doubt me, little policeman?" Rémy shouted back.

He stared at her, half circus imp and half drowned rat. "Never," he said. "I never did."

"Catch," she shouted, tossing the Ocean in an elegant arc.

Thaddeus caught the diamond two-handed, putting it into his pocket and reaching down to hold out a hand. "Come on," he said. "There'll be another wave. Get up here!"

But Rémy did not take his hand. She was already reaching back through the narrow gap of broken glass, trying to reach the second diamond.

"Leave it!" Thaddeus told her, glancing out the door. He could see another wave building, bigger than all the others. "Rémy, just leave it there!"

She shook her head, her fingers stretching toward the stone.

"Rémy!"

She wouldn't listen. He wasn't even sure if she could hear him, so intent was she on the diamond that was almost within her reach. Thaddeus scrambled back down the sphere, but before he could touch even her shoulder, a new torrent crashed over them both.

He tried to grab her, but the water tore them apart instantly. It blinded him, filling his lungs as he clung to the sphere. He felt more glass splintering under him as the structure began to disintegrate. He tried to turn toward Rémy, his lungs burning for air, but the force of the water was too great to resist.

And then he felt it sucking at him. The wave rushed back out of the power chamber, hissing like a giant snake. It slopped past Thaddeus's ears, the echo of the room returning like a deafening gurgle. He reached one hand up to wipe his hair out of his eyes.

"Rémy," he croaked, when he could breathe. "Rémy . . ."

But she was gone, sucked into the chasm by the Black Ditch. It was as if she'd never even been there at all.

Chapter 22

MUDLARK'S
TREASURE

$\mathcal{R}$émy knew she was going to die the moment her fingers wrapped around the unexpected stone.

It was ironic, really. One moment, she had a flash of inspiration — the knowledge that perhaps this was the answer to all her problems — and the next, she was being dragged under the water, the breath beaten out of her by a turbulent tide.

She tried to see Thaddeus, but when she could finally open her eyes against the torrent, Rémy realized that she wasn't even in the power chamber anymore. Instead, the water had carried her with it, out of the door, over the venomous edge of the chasm, down among the unforgiving rocks. She was hurled against the stones as one wave met another, crashing together with enough force to pulverize the remaining breath in her lungs, but not enough to make her let go of the diamond.

The water rushed along the chasm, unstopping, unstoppable, and with every fraction of a second, Rémy's life faded out of her. She felt her opal tugging at her neck, the gem floating upwards, free of her body, tethered only by the gold chain around her throat.

This is it, she thought absently. *I wonder what comes next. I wonder if Mama and Papa will be there to meet me? I wonder what they will look like —*

She hit something new, smoother — not rock. The water spun her over, turning her toward this new object, and she realized it was made of glass. A glass dome, smooth, large, and as she blinked, inside Rémy saw a face. It was fixed in a scream as Abernathy's great submarine sank toward the bottom of the chasm, as dead and powerless as granite.

Rémy smiled, relief flooding through the blackness engulfing her mind. They really had succeeded. They really had stopped Abernathy's diabolical plan.

She sank like a stone thrown into a deep, deep pool, the blackness swallowing her whole.

And then there was nothing.

* * *

The first time Rémy woke, she thought she was dead. Then a voice seemed to echo deep in her head.

Poor girl, it said, now seeming very far away — like a whisper that almost wasn't there at all.

Was she dead?

Poor girl. Poor girl . . .

Then Rémy felt something. Air on her face. She tried to breathe. She could. She gasped.

Suddenly, there was noise. It rushed into her mind, drowning her senses. The wind, and something else. Something cracking sharply against something else, *chink-chink-chink.*

Not dead, said the voice, like a whisper, below the noise.

Rémy tried to open her eyes, but the light was too bright. She screwed them shut.

Something touched her arm.

Tide coming, said the voice. *Tide coming, got to move.*

The light outside her eyelids grew dimmer. She opened her eyes into the shadow of a person. It was an old man, leaning over her. His face was lined and twisted. He wore a hooded cloak, pulled up over his bald and ailing head. He jumped back as she moved.

"W-what?" she managed. "W-what did you say?"

He shook his head and remained at a distance, staring at her. Rémy blinked into the sooty sunlight. She was staring at a gray sky studded with heavy clouds. She turned her head, and grit pressed itself into her ear. Sand. She was lying on sand. Water was lapping, gently, at her feet.

I know this place, she thought. *I have been here before.*

She was lying on the Thames river shore. There were boats moored against the edges of the bank built out in the middle of the dirty water. They were bobbing, the wind moving their mid-sails against their dormant masts. Rémy tried to move but a great weariness engulfed her. She curled up on her side instead right there on the sand, coughing as her lungs struggled with the effort of taking in air.

Tide, said the old man's voice again, except that it didn't sound like a voice, because it came to her from somewhere deeper than her ears. Like an idea, or . . . or a thought. She turned her head again, squinting up at him. He had taken hold of her arm and was trying to pull her up. *Tide — tide.*

"Louder," she rasped. "Say it — louder."

He shook his head and pointed at his mouth. For the first time, Rémy noticed that it was twisted and misshapen, incapable of forming words.

She didn't know how he seemed to be speaking to her when he obviously couldn't, but she struggled to her feet, leaning on him heavily.

"Home," she said, her voice fading away as the tiredness sucked her down into darkness once again. "C-circus. Claudette. Yes?"

The old man nodded but said nothing. They made it up the rickety steps to the roadside before Rémy let the blackness take her once more, sinking to her knees and then the ground, and then into oblivion again.

★ ★ ★

The second time Rémy woke, it was into a blur of noise and movement and musty cloth. There was shouting, the sound of horses' hooves. Rain was falling on her face but not on the rest of her, as if she was lying face up on a moving piece of earth, buried in blankets. She tried to lift her shoulders, but someone pushed her back down. She passed out again.

★ ★ ★

The final time Rémy woke, the rain had gone and she heard a voice. It was talking quietly at some distance. She recognized it.

"C-Claud . . . Claudette?" she whispered.

There was a gasp and the sound of quick movement. Into Rémy's clouded vision stepped a shadow. Rémy blinked, but the lights were dim and her eyesight was blurred. She felt a soft hand stroke her forehead. She smelled the perfume that Claudette insisted on buying, even when she had no bread to eat.

"Praise be," Claudette murmured. "Oh, my Little Bird, praise be, praise be. I was not sure you would awaken at all. No — don't try to move . . ."

But Rémy wanted to sit. With Claudette's help, she lifted herself up and leaned against the wall. She was in Amélie's bunk in Claudette's caravan. She was home. She reached out to her friend, and Claudette wrapped warm arms around her, kissing the top of her head.

"You have been on a great adventure, Little Bird, I think. Have you not?"

Rémy nodded, her eyes focusing enough to see Amélie, regarding her seriously from the little table across the narrow room. In front of the child was spread a picture book — the alphabet. Claudette had been giving her a lesson.

"What is the time?" she asked.

"Just beyond eight of the clock," Claudette told her, pulling away slightly to brush the hair from Rémy's face.

Rémy frowned. "I can't hear anything."

Claudette looked a little alarmed. "You don't hear me speak?"

"No . . . no — I mean, the circus? Why can I not hear noise from the big top?"

Her friend smiled, shifting slightly to settle them together more comfortably. "Little Rémy, always thinking about work. There is no circus tonight. Nor was there last night, nor the night before."

"What — what do you mean? What about Gustave? He never stops the circus, he never —"

"Shh," said Claudette. "There is no Gustave. The police came and took him away. We are free, little one. I have been running the circus since he went, but when you were returned to us, almost dead . . . well, I had more important things to worry about, yes? You have been asleep for a long, long time. So we . . . are having a holiday. The whole company needs it."

Rémy blinked, trying to take all of this in. No Gustave? No Gustave ever again? "But . . . the police?"

Claudette pushed her back, gently, against the pillows. "Do not concern yourself, Rémy. Not now. You need to get strong again, to rest. There is some soup left from dinner, I will heat it for you."

Rémy held on to her arm, before she could move

away. "Wait," she said. "Wait — the policeman. The policeman who came to take Gustave. Was it — was it Thaddeus? Was it Thaddeus Rec?"

Claudette frowned. "Thaddeus?"

Rémy swallowed, a painful lump in her throat. "The little policeman. The one who came the night I had to flee. Was it him, Claudette? Have you seen him?"

The older woman shook her head. "No. He has not been here at all, Little Bird. Not since that night. There was a great flood, not far from here. The police have been far too busy to come looking for you. Do not worry. You need to rest."

Rémy felt tears fill her eyes. She sank back and turned her head away, because looking at her friend was too much. Then she remembered the diamond. The one she had been reaching for as the water whirled her away.

"My jacket," she mumbled. "The jacket I was wearing. Did you find it? Was there . . . was there anything?"

"Ah," said Claudette. "I believe you may be wondering about this, yes?"

Rémy turned back to see her friend holding up the gemstone in her palm. Claudette had polished

it, and it shone like a beautiful beacon in the dim
room.

"When you are better, *ma chérie*," said Claudette as
she put down the jewel and opened the caravan's door,
"I think you may have a very big story to tell. I will be
back with food."

She left, closing the door softly behind her. Amélie,
ever the silent child, got up from her chair and crossed
the room, climbing onto the bunk and curling up.
Rémy pulled her close and buried her face in the girl's
mass of curly hair.

"Did you miss me, little one?"

Amélie nodded.

Mommy sad without you. Amélie sad without you.

Rémy raised her head. Amélie had never said a
word in her entire life.

"Did you — did you speak, Amélie? Has mommy
taught you how?"

The child shook her head, blue eyes blinking at
Rémy curiously.

No. I don't. Can't.

Rémy stared at her for a moment. And then a
thought sped into her mind, so fast that it made her
heart thump. She fumbled at her throat, beneath her
bed shirt, until she felt the gold chain that was always

there. Pulling it out, Rémy peered at the opal. Its colors seemed brighter somehow, and it had cracked, a furrow lying through its center as surely as if someone had cleaved it with an axe. She remembered what Desai had asked her, what seemed like a lifetime ago. *Have you ever been able to hear the thoughts of others? In your head?* And hadn't he said it might have been sleeping? What could wake a stone? Rémy turned cold, a shiver working its way down her spine. She hid the opal under her bed shirt, determined not to think about it. It was all too strange to comprehend.

★ ★ ★

A few days later, just as the circus was packing up, Rémy had a visitor. There was a knock on the caravan door as Rémy was lying in bed, playing checkers with Amélie on a makeshift board. Claudette opened the door and there was Desai, his head almost brushing the ceiling. Behind him, dressed more cleanly than she had ever seen him, was J.

Rémy leapt out of bed and flung her arms around them both, far more quickly than was wise given her still-feeble condition.

"*Mon Dieu!*" she said, as Desai helped her back to bed. "How did you know I was here? I was going to come looking for you, but I have been so tired . . . I was planning, when I was better . . ."

Desai smiled his gentle smile and patted her on the shoulder. "That is why we came to you, my dear girl. It was J who found you."

"Took me a while, it did," J told her. "But I reckoned there was a good chance you weren't dead. 'Not our Rémy Brunel,' I said. 'She's too brave to die,' I said. So I went 'round and about, to see if anyone 'ad 'eard anyfing, like."

"I — I washed up on the riverbank," Rémy said. "There — there was an old man."

J bobbed his head. "Aye — the mute mudlark. Tha's right. 'E told me where you were. Well, I say told. 'E scratched it down, see. In the sand. 'Home,' it said. 'Circus.' And tha's when I knew it was you. It ain't 'alf good to see you, Rémy."

Rémy returned his grin, though hers was overlaid with sadness. Seeing J reminded her of Thaddeus and she didn't want to think about the watery death he must have suffered, waiting for wave after wave until that tiny cave was full.

"What are people saying, Desai?" she asked instead, when she knew she could speak without tears. "About what happened? Claudette said there was a flood."

"People assume that there was a storm out at sea," he told her, "and that it caused the Thames to be higher than usual and break its banks. It happens."

Rémy nodded, twisting her fingers together. "And Abernathy? His men? What happened to them all? When I was in the chasm, I saw . . . I saw one of the submarines, lying dead. But what about the rest?"

Desai and J glanced at each other. "We have been looking," he said, "for any trace of the madman and his men. But there is no sign that any of his people or their contraptions escaped. I think — I think we must be grateful for that."

There was a moment of silence as they all thought about Abernathy's vast army, lost beneath the streets of London.

"I had a — a reason for wanting to see you again, Desai," Rémy said after a moment. "Besides wanting to know if you were all right, I mean."

"Oh?"

Rémy fumbled beneath her pillow and pulled out the diamond, wrapped in an old rag. J gasped as she held it up. "It was with the Darya-ye Noor. In Abernathy's power chamber."

Desai reached out and took it with a frown, turning it over in his palm as the diamond flashed in the light.

"It is a valuable one," Rémy said quietly. "I can tell, just by looking at it. There are no flaws in it. It is cut in the old style, so it must be ancient."

The Indian looked up at her. "You are right on all counts, Rémy Brunel, oh knower of gems. But there is something else. Something you may not know."

Rémy looked away. "I think I do. It's the stone, isn't it? It's the stone my parents stole. The one they were cursed for. Abernathy had it all along; it just wasn't powerful enough for his plan. Am I — am I right?"

Desai nodded. "Yes. Yes, you are right."

"I knew," Rémy whispered, staring at the beautiful glow of the jewel that had destroyed her parents. "I knew as soon as I saw it."

There was a silence. Desai continued to turn the diamond over in his hand. "I can return this for you, Rémy," he said quietly into the hush. "I can go to India and give this to its rightful owner. The curse would be lifted. You would be free."

Rémy smiled sadly and nodded. "I know," she said. "But . . . but that doesn't really seem very important now. And I was thinking — I was thinking that perhaps we should present it to the Shah of Persia. To replace the Darya-ye Noor. Do you think? Would that — would that be the right thing to do?"

What she really meant to ask was, "Is that what Thaddeus would have wanted?" but Rémy couldn't bring herself to say his name.

Desai looked at her with a frown. "That is a very noble gesture, Rémy."

"Be a bit greedy of him, though, wouldn't it?" J piped up. "'E of all people don't need two big stinkin' gemstones, do 'e?"

"Two?" Rémy asked, puzzled.

"Yeah. If 'e's goin' to 'ave the Ocean o' Light, why does 'e need this one, too?"

"But — but the Ocean of Light was lost, wasn't it? When the power chamber flooded. It was lost, with, with . . ."

J laughed. "Pfft. You fink Mr. Rec was going to leave it there, after all the trouble 'e went to get it? You must be jokin'!"

Rémy shook her head. Her heart was doing strange things in her chest. "But — but Thaddeus — Thaddeus is dead. Isn't he? There — there was no way out of that room. Except, except down the chasm, like me, and I only just survived that, so . . . so . . ."

"Mr. Rec, dead?" cried J. "I surely 'ope not, Rémy, or I been tending to a ghoul the past week!"

Rémy felt the blood drain from her face. Desai

leaned forward and grasped her shoulder. "The very excellent Thaddeus Rec is far from dead, Rémy. He has been in hiding, yes. He has needed almost as much care as you, though I think his wounds have been less physical and more of the mind. But he is alive, my dear. He is well. We would have brought him here, but when J learned of your whereabouts, Mr. Rec had taken himself off to perform an errand of his own, and J could not wait for him to return before seeing if it really was you."

J jumped up. "It was right bad o' me, that, I know," said the boy, "but I'll go right now and get 'im. We've been staying at the Professor's old workshop, y'see. 'E must be back by now —"

"No," said Rémy hoarsely, cutting him off. "No, J. Don't. Don't."

Silence fell again as J and Desai both looked at her.

It was Desai who spoke first. "What is it, Rémy?"

She shook her head. "He — things did not work so well for him when I was alive. Perhaps it is better if he thinks I am dead. I will go back to France, out of his life, and he can go back to being the good policeman, without me."

Desai smiled and shook his head. "Surely, Miss Brunel, you must know that cannot be the case."

Rémy drew a deep breath, her mind made up. Then she frowned as a thought occurred to her.

"So, he has given the Ocean of Light back?"

"Not yet 'e ain't. 'E 'asn't been well enough, and 'e wouldn't let no one else do it for 'im. Nah — that's where 'e's gone just now. 'E was off to 'is old station. They're going to get a right shock when 'e walks in there with that diamond!"

Rémy shot to her feet. "But — but he can't! He can't do that!"

J frowned, puzzled. "Why not?"

"Because they still think he stole it! They think — they think it was him, all along!"

"Nah," J said doubtfully. "Not Mr. Rec. They wouldn't, would they? Not after everything . . ."

"They don't know about everything else!" Rémy cried. "And they won't believe him if he tells them, will they? It is too — too ridiculous. All of it! They will arrest him! They will — they will blame him!"

"Oh, no," said J, growing pale. "You're right!"

Rémy spun toward Desai. "He would have known that. He can't have not known that!"

Desai nodded solemnly. "I think he probably did."

Rémy grabbed her street clothes and began to pull them on. "I can't let him do it. I can't . . . I can't let him throw his life away, his career. He'll go to prison!"

She hardly took any notice as Desai stood and motioned to J that they should go.

"J and I have a long trip to take, Rémy," he said softly. "Will you be well without our assistance?"

"Yes," Rémy replied, hardly listening. "I just — I just have to stop him. I'll see you soon."

"Perhaps," said Desai, then he bowed to her and left.

It was only as she was rushing along Wapping High Street that Rémy realized he had not handed back the diamond.

{Chapter 23}

A CAGED BIRD

$\mathscr{I}$t was raining again, icy drops pouring from London's indolently melancholic sky. Thaddeus Rec pulled his collar up and then realized it was possible that after today, he would not feel the rain for a very long time. He pulled it down again, letting the torrent run down his cold neck and savoring the feeling.

The past two weeks seemed to have lasted a lifetime and, when he thought about it now, he couldn't quite remember the man he had been before they began. He knew he was different. He knew he was older. He knew there was now a space in his heart that would never be filled again.

J had been so attentive — making him eat, making

him drink. Thaddeus himself would have been happy to let his life fade away, as he'd hoped would happen when he allowed himself to be taken into the chasm. But he suspected Desai had been slipping a concoction into his food that meant no matter how little Thaddeus wanted to, he had slowly regained his strength.

Even when he'd been at his weakest, though, Thaddeus had known what he had to do. The Shah of Persia deserved to have his stolen property returned, and the only person to do that was Thaddeus himself. He knew it would probably mean spending the rest of his life behind bars. But at the moment, he couldn't see the point of being free. His sleep was still haunted by the sight of Rémy's tiny frame being sucked beneath a volume of water so great it could have annihilated London itself, let alone a sixteen-year-old girl.

Finding himself on the street opposite Scotland Yard, Thaddeus paused. He remembered how he had looked forward to entering those doors each morning. Now he knew that, once inside, he faced the disdain of his peers. He put his hand into his pocket, feeling the Darya-ye Noor resting there safely, wrapped in yesterday's newspaper.

But, he thought, *there are worse things in life. And this*

is the right thing. All he'd ever wanted to do was the
right thing.

He took a deep breath and stepped out to cross the
road. Something hit him in the side. It was a person
with a hood pulled up over their head, tackling him so
hard that he almost fell over.

"What the —?"

"Idiot!" growled a voice. "What are you doing?
Stupid, stupid man!"

As Thaddeus looked down, his eyes fell on a face
that he thought he'd never see again. His mouth fell
open as the girl dragged him back to the curb and
along the street.

"Rémy?" he whispered. "Rémy Brunel?"

She stopped as they reached a small alley. She
pushed him into it, turning to look up at him. "Yes,
of course, me. Who else would care to stop you, little
policeman? Foolish man, what are you doing?"

He couldn't speak. He could hardly take a breath.

"What?" he whispered. "How . . . I mean, when . . .
How did you . . ."

She shook her head and stepped away from him,
glancing over her shoulder into the empty alleyway. "It
takes more than a little bath to kill me, Thaddeus Rec.
But you — you. How did you survive?"

He stared at her, trying to fathom how she was here, now, in the flesh, as whole and as angry as she ever had been.

"I — I don't know," he told her, truthfully. "Maybe — maybe because I didn't want to."

She didn't seem to have anything to say to that, so Thaddeus reached out and pulled her to him, wrapping his arms around her. Her face pressed into his neck. After a second, she held on to him, too.

"I thought you were dead," he said, and the words were so terrible that they still made him tremble.

She nodded, her hair brushing his cheek. "I thought you were, too. Instead you were just being stupid, as usual."

He pulled away. "What do you mean?"

"J says you are taking back the Darya-ye Noor."

"I have to. It belongs to someone else."

She slapped a hand against his shoulder in frustration. "Agh! They will arrest you!"

"I know that."

"Then let me. Let me take it in. I can be your prisoner. You can prove that it wasn't you!"

He was taken aback. "I'm not doing that!"

"Why not?" Rémy cried. "It's true!"

"It's not true! Abernathy took it, not you!"

"But only because I didn't get there first! This is my fault. This is all — all my fault." He tried to pull her close again, but she shook him off and stepped away. "I can't let you take the blame, Thaddeus. You — you changed me. You know? You — you made me want to . . . to do the right thing. And you going to prison, for me or Abernathy — that is not the right thing."

Thaddeus smiled. "It is. It is the right thing. It's —"

Rémy threw herself at him, wrapping her arms around his neck and pulling his head down to hers. Their lips met before his heart even realized what was happening. He went into free fall as a thunderbolt hit him, burning white-hot, straight through to his core. The kiss was soft and urgent at the same time, and he pulled Rémy closer, backing against the wall of the alley and lifting her up until there was no space at all between them. He felt her slip her arms around him, running her hands up his back, down his arms, around his waist. Their mouths parted, met again, the kiss growing deeper and deeper.

Thaddeus didn't know how long it lasted, and he didn't care. When he lowered her to the ground again they were both out of breath. And then he realized that Rémy was crying.

"Rémy?" he asked. "What is it? What's the —"

She leaned in against him briefly, pressing another kiss to his lips, her tears touching his cheek. And then, before he could react, she ran.

"What? Wait!" he called as she fled out into the street. "Where are you going? What's wrong?"

Realization hit him like another thunderbolt, but this time it drove his heart through the floor. Thaddeus fumbled in his pocket.

The diamond. The Darya-ye Noor. It was gone. Only the newspaper was left behind.

"No!" he shouted, running after her. Rémy was already across the street and heading straight for the main doors of Scotland Yard. "Rémy!" he bellowed after her, dodging carts as he crossed the road. "Don't do it! Don't you —"

Thaddeus was only a couple of moments behind her, but he was already too late. By the time he'd burst through the wooden double doors of Scotland Yard, Rémy was surrounded by police. She was holding the Ocean of Light high above her head. "I can't take it anymore," she cried shrilly, and then pointed straight at Thaddeus. "He never gives up! He won't leave me alone until he's caught me! And now — and now he has! I give up! I surrender the stone. I give myself up!"

Thaddeus froze, out of breath, as every uniformed face turned to look at him. He saw Collins's ruddy face staring at him, the beginnings of surprised pride blooming in his eyes. And there was Chief Inspector Glove, looking fatter even than he remembered.

"Is this true, Rec?" Glove asked, stepping toward him with narrowed eyes.

Thaddeus shook his head. "No. Wait, I —"

"'Ere," spoke up Collins, peering closely at Rémy. "'Ere — I know this girl. She was there, sir! She was there, the night the diamond was nicked from the Tower. She 'elped that old man, she did, Lord Abernathy . . ."

Glove glanced at Rémy, looking her up and down. "Well. She certainly looks like trouble." He turned back to Thaddeus, staring at him coldly for a moment. Then the Chief Inspector reached out to slap him on the back. "Well, well, Rec, this is a turn-up for the books. It seems I owe you an apology, after all. Still, no hard feelings, eh? Good work, boy, good work."

Thaddeus took no notice of Glove's prattle. He was looking at Rémy. The Ocean of Light had been snatched from her hand, her arms pulled roughly behind her back. Collins was dragging her off to the cells.

"Wait," Thaddeus said. "Just — just wait. It was my arrest. Let me take her."

Collins looked askance at Glove, who nodded. "Of course, of course. Only fair. Have at it, Rec."

Thaddeus walked toward Rémy, taking her by the arm. Between them, he and Collins walked her down the stairs to the dank and dirty cell, not so very different from the worst parts of Abernathy's labyrinth. The only air down here came from the tiny windows high up in the cell walls, which lay at street level and were therefore always letting in dirt scuffed up by passers-by.

Collins chattered as they walked, but Rémy and Thaddeus did not speak a word. Thaddeus was trying to work out what to do, how to get her out of this mess. It didn't seem fair that it had come to this, not after he'd believed her dead. Not after he'd been so overjoyed to be proven wrong, about everything.

He had no choice but to slam the cell door and lock it behind her. He stared through the little window in the solid wood, willing her to look at him, as Collins' voice filled the corridor. Rémy glanced at Thaddeus once, a small smile lighting her eyes.

"Come on, lad," Collins said, as he lingered. "You've got some paperwork to do. And then we should celebrate. My treat, eh? A pint o' half-and-half on me, how about that?"

Thaddeus forced a smile. "That sounds good, Collins, thank you. I'm just going to get the girl some water. I — I chased her pretty hard, you know."

Collins nodded. "You always were more decent than people rightly deserved, Thaddeus. Come on, let's see what we can find. There might be a bit o' bread, too, if she's lucky."

She was gone, of course, by the time they got back. The cell stood empty, not a trace that she'd ever been in it. Not a trace apart from the broken glass of the tiny window, which every copper in the station swore blind was too high for anyone to reach.

They rushed to the circus ground — even the Chief Inspector — but the field was empty.

The circus had vanished. And with it Rémy Brunel.

THREE MONTHS LATER

*I*t had been a long, tiring day. Thaddeus Rec sighed and having finally finished his last report — for now — put down his pen and leaned back in his chair. Crime in London seemed to be on the increase, but Scotland Yard was determined to get it under control. They were recruiting more people — good people — and Thaddeus had taken a step up. He was an inspector now. Glove had obviously decided a promotion for Rec was the right way to go, what with the Shah of Persia's gratitude over the return of his diamond and Queen Victoria's personal interest in the case.

Thaddeus thought back to those days. How strange they had been, and yet how wonderful at the same time. Not only because of the dastardly plot they had uncovered and stopped under the streets of London — that secret that no one else would ever know — but also because of Rémy Brunel.

Thaddeus knew he would never meet anyone like her again. He wondered where she was at that moment. In a caravan, rumbling through France, no doubt, or on the trapeze, flying through the air. He'd started writing letters to police stations all over France. All he needed was a starting place, a town that she had passed through, perhaps. But there had been nothing useful yet. It was as if Le Cirque de la Lune had left Earth altogether and returned to the night skies. It was good his job was so busy. His work was important, and it kept him occupied. It stopped him thinking about the hole in his heart that had opened the day he realized she had gone away. But at least he knew she was alive and free. Wherever she was and whomever she was with.

There were worse alternatives, after all.

Pulling himself out of his reverie, Thaddeus sighed and stood up. He was reaching for his coat when there was a knock at the door.

"Come in!"

The door creaked open. "Mr. Rec?"

Thaddeus spun around, surprised to see J standing in the doorway.

"J!" the inspector exclaimed. "My God — J! I haven't seen you since the day . . . well, for months! I thought something terrible had happened to you!"

The boy grinned and moved further into the room. "To me, Mr. Rec? Not likely. I got a charmed life, I 'ave."

Thaddeus realized that J's face was dark and weathered, as if he had spent the last three months in foreign climes. "Where on Earth have you been, J? I've been looking for you!"

The boy tapped one finger to his nose and raised an eyebrow. "Need to know, Mr. Rec. But don't you worry. Me and Tommy, we had to help Mr. Desai wiv somethin', that's all. 'Ad to go a long way to do it, as well. But we're back now, in ol' London Town, and very nice it is to see the place, too."

"For Desai?" Thaddeus repeated, mystified. "It wasn't — it wasn't illegal, was it, J?"

J made a scornful sound in his throat. "Not likely. You won't catch me doing nuffin' bad no more, Mr. Rec. I'm getting h'educated, I am. Me an' Tommy, though it took 'im a while to get well enough, it did. The sun 'elped, though."

"Sun?"

The boy shook his head. "Never mind, Mr. Rec. I just came to see how you was, like. You look good."

Thaddeus nodded, looking down at his desk. "I am good, J. Mostly."

They were silent for a moment, and Thaddeus wondered if J was thinking about Rémy, too. He was about to ask the boy a question, when he piped up.

"Well, I got to be going, anyway, Mr. Rec."

"Oh — but you only just got here. Don't you want some dinner, or something? My treat."

J grinned and patted his stomach, which was definitely a shade bigger than the last time Thaddeus had seen him. "No fanks, Mr. Rec. I'm not wantin' for food no more. I've got to run an errand right now. But maybe another time, eh?"

"Right," said Thaddeus, faintly disappointed. "Right, of course."

The boy turned and made to leave. But then he paused for a moment, halfway out of the door.

"'Ere," he said. "You ain't into theater, are yer?"

"Theater?" Thaddeus asked, mystified for the second time in ten minutes. "No — no, not really. Not my thing, generally speaking. Why?"

J nodded. "It's just, there's this place. Down East. A

theater. They've got this new act. Been there the last two, three months, they say."

"Oh?" Thaddeus reached for his pen, wondering what on Earth J was talking about and why the boy thought he'd be at all interested.

"Yeah," J went on, his voice studiously nonchalant. "Really different, she is. She — she walks on wire and stuff. You know — high up. Off the stage, like."

Thaddeus froze, his hand halfway to his pen. He looked up at J, who shrugged, a twinkle in his eye.

"They say it's like she's flying, Mr. Rec. Like she's flying, only she don't need wings, see. She's that good."

Thaddeus coughed, and realized he hadn't been breathing. "What — where is this?"

"It's called the Albert Saloon, Mr. Rec. Down Hoxton way. Bit of a rough place, it is. But it's a good show, so they say."

Thaddeus felt a sweat break out on his forehead. He looked for the right words. "Is it — God, J, is it . . ."

The boy turned away. "I got to go now. Things to do. But I'll see you soon, yeah? Meanwhile, maybe you should take the night off, like. Enjoy yourself."

Thaddeus stared at the doorway long after J had left.

★ ★ ★

It was different, Rémy thought to herself, performing on a stage instead of in a tent. For one thing, it was smaller and, for another, it had taken a while for her to remember that the audience was only in front of the stage, not all around.

She stood on the plunge board that the Albert Saloon had built especially for her and waited for the music. The act before her was puppets. Well, a kind of puppet, anyway. It was a ventriloquist act, which she didn't really like, but the man behind it, Mr. Jones, was nice enough.

All her new friends were nice enough. She missed the circus, especially Claudette and Amélie, obviously, and her pony, Dominique, but Rémy loved London now. She loved the permanence of it. She'd thought at first that audiences would get bored of her if she was in one place too long. But she just needed to pull out a few new moves every so often, and they seemed to be happy. And anyway, she wasn't on every night. Twice a week, that was all. The management wanted to keep her a secret, almost, or at least just for the locals. They were worried that if she became too popular, one of the big West End theaters would offer her more money and fame.

But Rémy didn't want fame. She was happy being anonymous. She was happy in hiding. After everything, she thought it was for the best, even though there was one person she had to stop herself going to see, every day. But she'd caused so much trouble, and maybe he didn't . . . maybe he wouldn't . . .

Her music started, and Rémy batted those thoughts away as she adjusted her mask. It was a new addition, made of the most beautiful feathers that Rémy had ever seen. They had been a present from Desai and J, who had brought them back from India. J had taken great pleasure in describing the bird they had come from. Like nothing he'd ever seen before, the boy had said. He hadn't known that birds such as peacocks had even existed before he went to Desai's homeland.

Rémy smiled to herself at the memory. Then she counted a beat and slipped out into the air, spinning on her rope. This was a new trick, one that she had learned especially for the stage. She let herself drop sharply, turning over until she was falling headfirst, hearing the crowd gasp as she flew low enough that her hair brushed the floor. Then she twisted up again, winding the rope around her foot until she was upright, one leg thrown out as if she were pirouetting like a ballerina, arms free.

Someone caught her eye. It was a man in the first row. He wore a long brown coat and a battered top hat, and he was so familiar from her dreams that the world drew to a halt.

Little Bird, he thought, so clearly that it was as if he'd whispered it into her ear. *I would know you anywhere. My Rémy. Rémy Brunel.*

He looked at her with eyes that were the most beautiful she had ever seen, all the more so for being so completely mismatched.

One blue, like the sky over Paris on a sunny day.

One brown, like good chocolate.

Thaddeus Rec.